Weird Luck Tales No. 8

Edited by

Andrew M. Reichart

Weird Books for Weird People

Argawarga Press is an imprint of Autonomous Press that publishes genre fiction, with a focus on themes of weirdness and neurodivergence.

Autonomous Press is an independent publisher focusing on works about neurodivergence, queerness, and the various ways they can intersect with each other and with other aspects of identity and lived experience. We are a partnership including writers, poets, artists, musicians, community scholars, and professors. Each partner takes on a share of the work of managing the press and production, and all of our workers are co-owners.

ISBN: 978-1-945955-32-7.

Cover art and interior illustrations by Matthew Jaffe.

Cover design by Clint Marsh.

Book design by Casandra Johns.

Contents

Whale Song

Ross T. Byers

Dynamiting the beached whale was a bad idea. It had washed ashore dead but intact, though since its appearance it had swollen to twice its initial size, the trapped gasses of its decomposition ballooning it. It lay there on its side, not moving, not breathing, its great mouth hanging open to expose its teeth and tongue. Its skin was necrotic gray. Seagulls flocked to it, and a horde of crabs crawled over it at all hours of the day. And the number of flies it drew! If the townspeople could have seen its eye, which was once milky white (such a view was impossible from the beach, since the eye was pointed at the sky and the whale, even on its side, was taller than the tallest person in town), they would have seen that it had become a sort of maggot soup.

It was peak tourist season, and the corpse of the leviathan marring their otherwise pristine white beach was something the townsfolk couldn't have. A meeting was held to determine what was to be done with the whale corpse. Someone proposed that they use some of the old sticks of dynamite left over from the days when the town supplemented their earnings from fishing with a small mining operation a few miles inland. In theory, if enough explosives were used they would simply disintegrate the unsightly corpse. The city council voted unanimously to approve the use of dynamite.

The town advertised the whale removal as a sort of festive event, a one time experience that land-locked tourists wouldn't want to miss. Even citizens of the seaside town came out in droves to watch. A beached whale was an uncommon occurrence, this being the first in any living townsperson's memory, and no one had ever seen one explode before. So it was a goodly sized crowd gathered that day to watch, with the locals somewhat outnumbered as was the usual case during tourist season.

No less honorable a personage than the mayor himself set off the detonation. He stood before the box, its plunger raised like an upper-case T, the stiff breeze blowing in from the sea (carrying with it the scents of brine and rot) making the coattails of his old-fashioned suit billow and flap like pennants. The engineer once again assured everyone that they were all standing a safe distance from the explosives. The mayor smiled and waved at the gathered crowd, his teeth glistening in the sunlight, his walrus mustache bristling. He tipped his bowler hat to his wife and children, then depressed the plunger.

The whale's head disappeared in a red plume. The sound of the blast washed over the crowd, and there was just enough time to begin a cheer before they were pelted with blood and chunks of rancid whale meat. After a shocked pause, people started screaming. Children wept. From above came the cries of indignant ocean birds. The mayor hunched his shoulders, looking as though he wanted to shrink and disappear into his bowler hat as the bloody blubber rained down. The explosion had removed the whale's head but left the rest of it on the beach, its tail still curving into the surf, broken ribs poking up from the raw, red ruin. Liquefying organs spilled onto the sand. The breeze from the sea grew stronger, wafting the stench of putrefaction over the crowd. Tourists vomited their rich seafood lunches down their shirt-fronts, the stench of their sick mixing with that of the rancid meat.

Livid, the mayor berated the engineer. The crowd turned away, stunned, nauseated, disgusted, and trudged back to their homes and motel rooms. Families and lovers fought bitterly over who would shower first. Within the hour the town's only laundromat was overrun with tourists who desperately wanted to wash the whale blood out of their Hawaiian shirts and summer dresses. They squabbled over the washing machines, some still with blood and strings of meat clinging to their hair. And no matter how long they showered or how many times they ran their clothes through the wash, the stench of the dead whale clung to those who'd gathered on the beach to watch, as though their brief contact with its remains had made it a part of them.

The wind, relentless and remorseless, blew the stench of rot emanating from the exploded whale, so much worse now that it was opened up to the air, through the small seaside town so even those who hadn't been witnesses on the beach choked and gagged. People slammed shut their windows and doors in an effort to keep the stench out, but the wind found its way into homes, through the smallest cracks, carrying the malodor with it. The smell was inescapable, and the grocery store and filling station soon ran out of deodorizers. Their lack of availability inspired more fighting among the residents and tourists. Masks and handkerchiefs were the next items to disappear.

When the sun set, the townspeople and tourists retired to their homes and rented rooms, some of them bloodied and bruised. They ate their dinners, all of which tasted slightly of rotting whale. Soon they went to their beds, exhausted and sick. They slept. They dreamed.

This is when the whale song began, after the last person in the seaside town finally drifted off to sleep. Everyone in the town heard it in their dreams, for dreams are the medium through which the dead most easily communicate with the living. All of the dreams in which the song was heard were uniformly dark and cold. But for those who had been on the beach earlier that day to witness the detonation, those who were touched by the blood, the song was stronger. For them it was an irresistible summons, drawing them like a siren's song.

The mayor and his family, the engineer, the tourists and the townsfolk who had formed the crowd of witnesses rose from their slumber. They did not pause to dress before stepping outdoors, shuffling down the streets in the nude, in their skivvies, their pajamas, or, in the mayor's case, in an old-fashioned nightshirt and nightcap. Their eyes were open but dull and glassy, only vaguely comprehending. They shuffled like sleepwalkers, though once in a while one of their limbs would jerk violently as though they were a puppet with the string yanked too hard. They made their way down the streets to the beach, to the blasted, stinking remains of the whale.

They stood in front of the gory corpse for a while, listening to the song. Some of them swayed in place. All of them stared at the whale's remains. Then the first of them climbed into the red ruin where the whale's head used to be, using the protruding, broken-off bones for purchase. The others swarmed up after her. The first plunged her arm up to the elbow in the soft meat, curling her fingers around one of the large ribs. The others also clung to the whale at first, but then they were only able to grip each other. They swarmed and crawled and clung, shoulders pressing into stomachs into thighs into backs into heads into armpits into rears into elbows, no space wasted as they each wedged themselves into position. Once they were all in place they resembled, exactly, the whale's lost head, down to the open jaw and limp tongue. Some of those on the bottom had their faces pressed into the surf, but they didn't mind as the water washed down their throats to their lungs. Or, if they did mind, they weren't able to do anything about it.

It didn't take long after the sun rose for the townsfolk and tourists who had gone to the beach to be discovered. Lovers and spouses woke to find their loved ones missing from their beds. Mothers opened the doors to their children's rooms to find them empty. Calls to neighbors and the police yielded nothing. The wind had changed direction and no longer blew the stench of the whale inland, and a group of enterprising townspeople headed down to the beach to both see if they could find the missing people and figure out a way to dispose of the rest of the whale. Their reactions upon seeing those who had gone missing in the night recreating the whale's head were at first a sort of stunned silence, then cries of alarm and concern. They spoke to those who were clinging so tightly together, tried to shake them and pry them apart, but all their efforts failed. They were part of the whale, and the whale was dead.

The entity referred to as Ross T. Byers seeped into this reality during a rare celestial convergence. Quickly realizing the guise of horror author was the perfect cover while it went about its great and terrible task, it soon patched together a skin suit and has walked among you ever since, sowing nightmares in the unwary populace through the medium of prose.

If you value your sanity, do not follow him on Twitter @RTByers or visit his website rosstbyers.com.

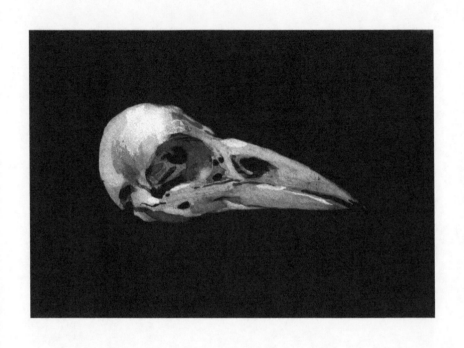

Birds

Zin E. Rocklyn

"Why do you ask for him ... when you know he ain't coming back?"

We were sitting on the couch, white shag carpet tickling the webs of my toes and her fingertips in my hair. Her touch was like dry ice, foreign and painful, yet warm to the point of hot and I'd been so, so cold, shivers still ran through me with each stroke. Still, I kept my face fused to the wide plain of her breast plate, like a tongue to the wall of a meat locker. I watched the rise and fall of her chest slow to the point of worry, my lips tingling for the feel of her suckle. I felt foolish, wanting my mother as if I were a babe. I was no more a babe than she was a mother.

"Why, Soot?" She was half-asleep and whole drunk, her words so lazy they melted into one. I shuddered, she sighed. "Why?"

I took a breath, fixed my tongue to answer, but then she pulled, her jagged nails digging deep into the forest of my kinks and she pulled hard, plucking follicles from the dry bed of my scalp and I counted each one, counted up to twenty-two and I screamed.

She stopped. Carefully removed each digit, taking one, three more with those long, serrated nails. She slid out from beneath me, behind me and stood up. Without her, I slid to the worn polyester, let the cilia tickle my cheek.

"Clean up this mess," she said, kicking over the quarter-full bottle of white wine before dragging her feet towards her room. I watched until the compressed wood shut her up for the night.

My body jerked in a familiar way as my fingertips gripped the wings of my shoulder blades. I rocked myself to sleep with a song I'd made up when my mom stopped singing to me, dreaming of a sky so black, no one could see me fly.

•

"You don't ask a snake why it slithers, it just does."

I angled the throw from my hip, like how he taught me, forefinger and thumb wrapped tightly along the short edges. I wound up, then released. Watched Mama's voice as it skipped along the brackish pond three, four times, then lost it.

"Nice toss."

I ignored her again. My dead sister was filled with riddles and I wasn't in the solving mood. I came here for my dead Pops and got her instead. The exchange wasn't much of a consolation.

I bent over for another stone, hoping for a smoother one, maybe a pale pebble of some kind, when I saw the ivory skull of a bird instead. My hand hovered above it, the contrast of my black-brown skin to the tea-stained white fascinating me into stillness. Couldn't name the bird, but it was small. The beak was long, about an inch and a half, the upper mandible slightly hooked, nostrils like uncovered tear drops of a small giant.

"What'chu got there?"

I heard her rising from the banks and I panicked a little, swiping at the skull and shoving it deep into my hoodie pocket before her heavy, ungainly steps could close in. Her cold reached me just as I dipped again for another stone. This one was sharper than the last, oddly shaped like a broken toy badge.

I grabbed it too quick, a jagged edge digging deep and hard and fast enough to smear my blood along its face.

Reminded me of my first fuck.

She kissed her teeth and I grit my jaw.

"Makes no sense, hiding shit from me," she said. "Just don't break it."

And suddenly I was warm again.

·

I was alone when I walked back through the sliding door, but the television was on full blast. Some daytime talking

head was shouting affirmations of self-worth and self-pres-
ervation when I pushed the dial in, the overly made-up face
collapsing into a horizontal blue pill before completely fading into a sandbag-settling silence.

To spite my mom, I walked through the white wine stain
with my muddy sneakers. She wouldn't buy me new ones,
despite the new year and a growth spurt, so I only hoped
my sore toes found as much satisfaction in this momen-
tary vengeance as I did. I had no idea where she or her boy-
friend was, but I didn't give a shit either. A moment like this
was rare and I had every intention of living in it.

I kicked off my sneakers and left them in the thresh-
old as I pushed open the door to my room and slid over to
the table that served as my desk, my bed being my chair. I
stripped off my dirty jeans and tossed them in a corner and
plopped down, bare-ass, on my comforter, carefully remov-
ing the skull from its polyester and cotton blend nest.

My hand shook as I laid the bone on the peeling varnish,
turning it slightly so the tiny baby-yawn eyeholes could
stare at me. I stared back for a solid minute before I felt a
shiver hammer its way down my back and I felt compelled
to push it away. I didn't, just got up instead and pulled on a
pair of sweatpants. The drawstring had to be pulled a little
tighter and I was doing just that when the air shifted, flut-
tered really, then trickled past my left cheek.

I shut my eyes and listened to the rustling, listened as
the plumage stretched to glorious lengths and heights and
in that moment, I could see it, I could feel that bird gaining
life and its desire for freedom.

I shouldn't have opened my eyes.

I should've let the theatre of dreams keep playing, keep going, keep projecting those pleasant beautiful images on the backs of my lids, but jealousy got the best of me. Pure envy made me open them, made me turn around to see the horror that was reality.

I didn't see much after. The plumage got in the way. So many feathers. So dark and full and opalescent as they caught every ray of sunshine that had dared to enter my tiny room.

It was upon me before I could even gasp with awe and the tinge of regret I'd known was bound to happen at the discovering of something so sacred.

The hook of the beak took my right eye first, leaving my left to watch as the baby raptor sat on my chest and opened its gullet, devouring the jelly as if it were a treat it had awaited forever.

Then it lowered itself to me, the tear-drop nostrils snorting thick spurts of air, the yawns of its eyes much larger now, like a void against yet another.

Still empty.

I joined that emptiness when the glint of the pointed beak kissed my remaining eye.

•

I came to with my sweatpants down to my ankles and my dead sister sitting on my bed.

"I told you not to break it," she said.

I blinked, sat up. Scratched my inner thigh. My nails came away with blood, brown and gummy. "I didn't."

"Taking it is breaking it, stupid. You should've left it alone."

I hated her riddles more now than in life. I wanted her to go away, but it wasn't that simple. It never was with the roaming dead.

"I need a favour."

"Another one." Statement. Fact. No riddles from me.

"Yes, another one."

"And then you'll leave me?" She was in my room, my sacred space, the one place she was never allowed. Their rules, not mine. Yet, I was the little sister again and screaming through balled fists for her to get out.

She blew out a breath, strands of hair with curls looser than mine drifting away only to fall right back. I wondered if this would be us forever. "Even scorpions need hugs."

"Fuck you."

She smirked, green eyes twinkling. "I need you to tell Daddy something."

I leaned over to my side, turf for carpet scratching my elbow, and dribbled a bit of sick. The stench filled the room quickly. I didn't think the dead could smell, but my sister's scrunched nose could've been habitual reaction. Muscle memory for disgust.

"Again, fuck you." I didn't bother wiping my chin.

"No one else can, stupid. Not even Mama."

"Worms must be eating that dead brain of yours. Your daddy ain't mine and he hasn't had a soft spot for Mama since he fucked her in the Caddy to make you."

She watched me. Waiting. Like only the dead can.

So I stood and pulled up my sweatpants. My shirt was on my sister's back. I said, "He spit in my face last time I saw him. Said I favoured Mama too much. Fuck makes you think he'll let me say a word?"

Then my sister smiled and my regret returned twice-fold.

"Sometimes what you break, breaks you."

•

Turns out my big sister knew exactly what she was doing, laying that bird skull on the rocky shore I visited daily. Ever since killing a baby bird nesting in my dead Pops' head, I'd been fascinated with them. I never killed another, but I'd collect their remains when I found them. Try to clean and keep them. Fail when the flies and beetles came for them, so I'd end up burying them somewhere near where Pops continues to rot in our yard.

It wasn't to see her so much as to live in the memories that still reside there along with her. The better ones, ones like my Pops teaching me how to skip a rock so it damn-near floats to the other side some two hundred feet away and how to shoot the .45 that eventually took his life. Like picnics and quick swims cuz there's worms that'll eat your future, you stay too long. It's the warmth, you see. They seek your warmth.

Either way, that bird was my sister's pet. And her portal.

After my Pops died, I used to stare at her for hours on end, wondering why we didn't have the same café au lait skin, the same rustled curls, the same bright gem eyes. Mama took to calling me Soot. Of course, my sister was fire. I was her remnants, the waste after the beauty burned bright.

After her soulless body with a bloated empty belly washed

up on that same shore, there was no flame to speak of. I didn't exist without my sister, incandescent shit or otherwise.

So it made sense that I'd have to become her to be seen.

•

With the weight of my sister's intentions sitting in me, I couldn't enjoy the spread of those wings as they split open my back, only the slightest twinge of discomfort registering as the ten-foot extensions lifted us up into the air. We landed on crow's feet, but walked in hers.

Her skin slipped from my frame once or twice, but settled well by the time we made it to the bottom of the winding drive. My sister was taller than me, but skinnier. Curves had no use on a beauty like hers, so my body ate up enough for the two of us. I was used to the oddity of it all once she knocked on the bleached oak door.

My sister's smile was painful when the door opened, yet the effort was futile once the maid recognized the infamous hair and eyes. Disbelief shoved the woman backwards, her skull glancing the corner of the hallway table with enough familiarity to crack it. A bright red slash stained the eggshell wall, dotted the mirror, muddied the entrance carpet.

My sister leaned over. Squeezed those ruddy copper cheeks. "No one's gonna believe you," she said, lips brushing the maid's forced pucker. The maid whimpered, shut her eyes against the familiar words, and my sister dropped her, let her crawl for the social room where the phone sat. But my sister waited until we witnessed the hesitation in the maid's pursuit. Watched as she touched the back of her head. Smiled as it all sat on her shoulders, weighing them down, hunching her back.

Satisfied, my sister went to her Daddy's study, found him standing in front of his books of law. Like the maid, he stumbled backwards when he saw her, hands scrambling for the shelves, desperate for purchase, slick with sweat. Unwieldy in their labours.

He fell hard on the flat ass my sister inherited, chapped lips parted as bursts of air wheezed past. Looked like a snake with its jaw forcibly unhinged for milking, spit for venom coating his chin.

"Daddy?" She tilted her head. My head. Our lips pouted and I stifled a giggle. For once, my sister's antics genuinely amused me. "Do you not recognize your baby girl?"

He tried, he really did. At least he looked like he wanted to try, wanted to speak and say yes, he knew her, always would know his baby girl, his little magpie, but the words wouldn't come. Not with his chest heaving the way it was, short and panicky, stumbling over itself, rippling unnaturally. His breath was trapped within, fighting to get out.

So my sister stepped forward and took one of his prized letter openers, the one with a raven as the handle, and she freed it for him.

"This little magpie just shit in your eye," she said, real close like. Her breath smelled of smoke and marsh. His of blood and dirt.

·

We found the key to the little boy's room in my sister's favourite book, some such nonsense about talking woodland animals with smarts that would one day match, then surpass her own. The room itself was a no more than a cubby, yet bigger than my own, situated behind those books of law. The boy was quiet, almost expectant when we met him sitting among toys he had no interest in.

He knew her face, but smelled me and it was the only way he'd come with us. I watched him close as my sister walked through the house. He was pale, like his father, but his hair was like my sister's. His eyes looked of both.

He was nothing like me or Mama.

Daddy finally had the scion he'd wanted.

•

Me and the boy were halfway home when the cruiser pulled alongside us, no lights other than the bright orange of the setting sun.

He was an officer I'd been familiar with and his pale face folded in on itself when he discovered I wasn't alone. He looked to the boy, then to me, then back again before saying, "Y'all alright?" His tone was stiff, hard. Resentful of such niceties.

I could still feel my sister in me, around us, but it'd been my face he was studying. My face he'd been looking for.

I squeezed the boy's hand gently when I heard him whimper, fixed my chin. Met his cold eyes. "We're fine."

My insides turned to acid mush as he looked us over, leaning over his empty passenger side, his radio squawking gibberish he paid no mind to. He was paying me thrice fold. My eyes flickered to the gleam of his tarnished badge and dread sat like an ice block in my belly as I briefly thought of our next, inevitable encounter. When I'd be alone. Without my sister. Without my brother.

The radio squawked again, the voice behind the static demanding attention. He tilted his head and spoke, eyes on me, thin chapped lips cutting into plastic as he responded. I squeezed my legs together a little tighter, my bladder knocking to let loose. A familiar address was spat back at him, a domestic disturbance it was called. Probably not a big deal.

I felt my sister just then, rippling just below the surface of my flesh. Felt her heat, her fire, her anger. The boy snatched his hand back and it was my turn to whimper.

The cop looked at us, saw her, then nodded briefly before driving away without another word.

·

We were alone when we walked in through the front door. The television was still off and not one light was on. Mama decided not to bother with me and my spite lay clumped and dried on the otherwise pristine shag rug. I decided to leave it, then crouched down to unstrap the Velcro closures to the generic superhero toddler sneakers. I kicked off my own, picked him up, and turned up the heat.

I put him on the counter, where he sat perched silent, watching me move around the kitchen with big blue-green eyes and sealed ruby-red lips.

I made us fried Vienna sausages and baked beans. He ate willingly, but only if I fed him.

I felt the corner of my mouth twitch upwards as I watched his battle of wills against sleep in a warm bath. I dried his skin and oiled some warmth into his bones before slipping one of my t-shirts over his head and a pair of shorts I couldn't let go of over his bum.

Not one word slipped past the lips so much like his mama's. My sister's.

But he didn't have to as I tucked him into my bed. His little fingers gripping my wrist with the strength of soul older than both of us told me all I needed to know.

I tapped the back of his hand twice and he let go. I showered and dressed and returned to the dark room to see those eyes illuminating one corner of my bed. I slipped in next to him at the edge of bed, to protect him from my desk, from that bird's skull watching us.

I slipped an arm around his middle and those nightlights shut tight, his soft breaths lulling me into a sleep of my own.

That night I dreamt of flying on the back of a magpie, my sister's laughter in my ears.

Of Trinidadian descent, Zin E. Rocklyn (she/they) is a horror and dark fantasy author hailing from Jersey City NJ. A contributor to several anthologies, including a non-fiction essay in the Hugo Award-winning *Uncanny Magazine's Disabled People Destroy Science Fiction*, the IGNYTE award-nominated writer is a graduate of 2017 VONA and 2018 Viable Paradise workshops. Their debut novella *Flowers for the Sea* was published by tor.com in October 2021. You can follow them on Twitter at intelligentwat.

And Neither Have I Wings to Fly

Carrie Laben

"I'm sorry," Faith said. A lie, but the satellite phone connection was too expensive to argue across. "The only safe thing to do is to stay put. We're well supplied, we're on the sheltered side of the island."

Vivian sighed. It was one with the wind against the porthole. "I wish you hadn't gone. Dad is worried to death."

I hope so. "This is my job. If I only went out when there couldn't possibly be a storm, I wouldn't go out at all."

"Yeah, but..."

"I have to go, Viv. Don't call again unless it's a real emergency, ok? I'll let you know as soon as we get back, promise."

"Ok." Faith had the phone halfway back to the cradle when she heard "One more thing!" She didn't hang up.

"What?"

"You'll never guess who I ran into the other day."

"No, I won't." The satellite phone was also too expensive to gossip across, but if she let Viv have this one moment maybe she'd save in the long run.

"Marika Mendel! Can you believe that? She came into the store, we had a nice chat." Viv pretended to catch herself. Or maybe it was honest. "But I know you can't talk long. I'll tell you all about it when you come home. Bye!"

Outside, the rain was just getting started, and most of the passengers -- five grad students, one professor, two amateur filmmakers, and three die-hard birdwatchers -- were still on deck, sucking up as much fresh air as they could, as though it'd last them through the storm. One of the filmmakers and one of the grad students had been seasick since they set out from San Diego as it was.

•

At night she wrote blog posts, even though she couldn't upload them until she reached shore. The blog was her best free advertising, and lots of good you-are-there material was the key to its appeal.

But that night, even though she should have been thinking of adjectives to make the storm sound like a glorious adventure that people would pay for, she wrote about gannets.

The Northern Gannet, Morus bassanaus, *is one of the largest seabirds of the north Atlantic. The adult bird is all white and ivory, except its wing-tips and feet which have been dipped in ink. Its beak is a spear...* no, backspace... *When it dives, it is a spear, its beak foremost. Flocks of gannets gather over schools of fish and plunge into the water from great heights, like bombs.*

She didn't write, *My mother is a gannet.* She never put personal stuff on the blog.

When she was done with the gannets, and with the little glass of Laphroig that helped her write, she walked back up on deck, to the lashing rain and the waves sending spray well over the deck. *If I had a skin of gannet feathers, this wouldn't bother me.* Her Marmot windbreaker was good enough, but the cuffs of her jeans got wet, and then dampened her socks.

Yet Vivian wouldn't even come out to sea. She said she wasn't scared, but Dad would never come -- Dad wouldn't even get in sight of the water, a beach scene in a movie made him walk out -- and she wouldn't leave Dad alone.

Faith suspected she was scared.

•

At the height of the storm a small yellow-and-black landbird tried to perch in the rigging, then fell to the deck exhausted. The birdwatchers hovered over it and identified it as a hermit warbler. It would break their rules to touch it, since nature must take its course, but they managed to crowd and shepherd it into the galley. The cook, Chaz, had been complaining about an infestation of fruit flies.

Chaz set a dish of water and some of the offending peaches on a counter. Out of the wind and the wet, the bird soon shed its sickly, puffed-up look and began to take an interest in these offerings.

Over dinner, everyone watched their new companion, who seemed to have more of an appetite than any human aboard. The sailors and the birders swapped stories of other warblers, sparrows, falcons, even a sand grouse that once washed on board an oil rig. The phalarope that flew into a lighted bathroom and swam in circles in the sink. The heron that crossed the Atlantic on a yacht.

When everyone drifted away and Chaz was washing up, Faith took a closer look at the bird. Almost certainly just a bird; still, on the off chance, she waited.

The bird ignored her, hovered to pluck a spider out of the corner, dropped back to the counter and drank. The yellow of its face shone in the slanting evening light. She could understand wanting to touch it, but she couldn't understand not knowing that touching it would be wrong.

Maybe she'd been hanging out with birdwatchers too much.

The bird stayed until the storm blew itself out and they started back for San Diego. Then one morning it was gone.

If it headed east, the birdwatchers said, it might make it.

•

Once they were back in range of port, Faith called Vivian. She tried to run through the usual reassuring niceties, but Vivian cut her off immediately.

"You're back?"

"Less than a day out of port."

"Thank god. We need your help on Wednesday; not tomorrow but this coming Wednesday, I mean."

"That's not going to work, I'm sailing out again as soon as we clean up and take on more supplies."

"I thought that you didn't have another trip scheduled for a month!"

"I didn't. But the director we took out this time got an inspiration and he's paying us to go out ASAP and get more footage. He wants to do a short feature on birds who get blown off-course and end up..."

"We need your help. An apartment in my building opened up and Dad's moving in. I can't keep driving back and forth across the city twice a day to check on him."

"That's great," Faith said. The idea made her choke. "You deserve more free time."

"And this way I can make sure he's actually eating real meals. You know how he is about cooking for himself."

"Well, it serves him right. He's had years to learn." Wrong, wrong wrong time for that argument, but too late to back up. "I'm sorry. I think it's a great idea if it makes things easier on you, but I'm heading out again by Monday at the latest."

"Tell the guy you have to wait."

"If I make him wait now, it'll be next year before he gets another shot at what he's looking for. And he'll probably go look for it with a different captain."

"We need you."

"No you don't. You'll be fine."

"With just my little car, it'll take two days."

"I didn't even known this would be happening."

"I didn't know that the apartment would be available."

"I'm sorry." It was a lie, but it was self-defense.

"Dad misses you."

There's nothing she could say to that, not even the baldest lie would fool Vivian into thinking that she felt sorry for Dad. Vivian heard silence, not the slap of the waves on the hull and the chatter of the passengers outside, and her own need to fill that silence would always push her on eventually. That was one of the few ways in which Vivian took after their father.

"I saw Marika again. In the store."

"How is she?"

"She's fine. I told her you'd be ashore this week, and that maybe you'd want to get dinner."

"Maybe next month."

"She probably won't be in town that long. She's only here to give a lecture at the university." Another pause. "She wrote a book, you know."

"No, I didn't know that. I always thought she was going to be an actress."

"It's about our situation. With, you know, our moms."

"Ah."

"I asked if we were in it, but she just laughed."

"Sounds like Marika."

"She'd probably tell you. If you were going to see her. But I guess you won't."

"I'll have to catch up with her another time."

"You always say things like that!"

"I'm sorry, I'm sorry." It didn't even feel like a lie anymore; it felt like a mantra. An incantation to protect her sister, and by extension herself.

She didn't go back to her own apartment during their brief time onshore, but stayed in a small hotel by the dock that normally catered to sport fisherman, where she could keep an eye on the repairs and restocking. She knew she should update the blog, at least upload a few photos, but it was easier to procrastinate on that. It wouldn't sink her.

On Saturday night, at 9:30, Vivian called again. She came within a single ring of letting it go to voicemail.

"Hello?"

"Guess what?" The joy in Vivian's voice told Faith that no one was in the hospital or dead. One more ring. Damn.

"No idea."

"Oh, come on, guess."

"You got a new job?"

"No, silly. Why would I be calling about a job this late on the weekend?"

"You heard from..."

"Mark proposed!"

Faith opened her mouth, but no sound came out. The first time she'd met Mark, he'd drunk all her beer and talked over her with stories about the 30-foot fishing boat he'd played around on with his dad in Sarasota, before his dad decided that being a bull was better than being a banker and a husband and a father.

"Tonight, at dinner. He had the waiter hide the ring in my dessert, it was so sweet, I started crying right there." She started crying again.

"Well, congratulations." That was ok. That sounded good.

"Look, I know you and Mark aren't best buddies. But I love him, and he really is a good guy if you'll give him a chance."

"If he makes you happy.... I want you to be happy." There. Something true and useful.

"I am! I'm so happy! Listen, here's what he wants to do. We're going to exchange skins. Instead of just him having mine, I'll have his too."

"That doesn't actually make it any easier if you split up."

"We're not planning to split up!"

"No one plans to split up."

"We won't do that. We both know what it's like, growing up with a parent who took their skin back and just took off. We wouldn't do that to our kids."

"Are you pregnant?" There was no keeping the oh-shit out of her voice.

"No! I'm just saying, when we do have kids, we have to both be in it for the long haul. And Mark knows that."

Don't say, but what if. Don't say it, don't say it.

"I'd like you to be my maid of honor."

Don't say, but what if.

"We're scheduling the wedding for July or August, you never go out then."

"Of course. Of course I'll be your maid of honor."

Vivian made a noise of delight, and for a moment Faith could feel the lure, the impulse that said, *making this other happy would be easier than making yourself happy. Making this other happy would replace making yourself happy.* But as soon as she felt it, she couldn't help thinking of the hook and how much thrashing it would take to get off of it.

"When you get back, we can talk about dresses and reception venues and things."

"Absolutely. When I get back." This time, she doesn't want to leave the silence hanging. "I know this is what you've been wanting. Congratulations, for real."

•

It was the first trip she ever ran where the passengers complained about the lack of storms. The director said, over and over again, that he knew he had to wait for the right moment, no different than any other documentary, especially when you're dealing with animals, that it was fine. She was starting to think he didn't believe it himself. His crew was antsy, counting dollars and days. Unlike the birders, or the people she sometimes took sport fishing, they weren't in tune with the kind of waiting the ocean required.

So when the bird appeared on the horizon, they damn near exploded. As it got nearer, Faith saw that it wasn't one of the normal Pacific birds she knew, and for a moment her heart rose up -- but it wasn't a gannet either, too big, and one of the few birds too white: a gannet would have black wingtips.

It was maybe the biggest bird she'd ever seen. Its long neck split the air as it headed straight for them, its long legs trailed behind it. She'd seen the image in a thousand photos and paintings, but she'd never seen a real crane, alive and flying free, before.

Without considering, without circling, it dropped for the deck and landed among them all. The director's crew scrambled to re-aim their cameras and get out of each other's shots. The crane gave an unbirdlike little shrug, shook its head. It was impossible to see how the feathers started to drop, even if you were watching for it; there was just a sort of rippling motion and then Marika Mendel stood there in the center of their circle with a trace of sweat on her forehead and a coat of birdskin bunched around her feet. She wore a pair of gray slacks and a black silk top, totally unsuitable for salt water, and sunglasses with huge green plastic frames, and the dangling feather earrings she'd had ever since Faith first met her at age twelve.

"Well," Marika said, glancing at the cameras as she scooped up her skin. "Looks like I came to the right place."

Faith shook her head. "This guy, he only wants birds who are in the wrong place."

"Bummer." Like all of them, she had the trick of folding her skin neatly without any apparent effort; it was a cube in her hands barely the size of a cigarette pack.

Faith knew she shouldn't stare at it. She should introduce Marika around. She should do a lot of things, and despite her surprise, she did -- made the introductions, showed Marika to an empty cabin and a head where she could wash up, gave her a quick overview of the ship's layout and where the life jackets were and when dinner was scheduled. All the while, she felt as though her brain was drifting somewhere a few feet behind her, still marvelling.

"So, you inherited the skin," she said when it finally caught up.

Marika nodded. "And so did Vivian, I hear."

"That's right."

"But..."

"But not me."

"Seems like it would have been better the other way around, though."

"You haven't changed."

"Sure I have. I've gotten taller, for one thing."

"I just heard the Marika who told Dr. Kravitz that her dad was just... what was it?... just fucked off that he couldn't go around with a Japanese chick on his arm anymore."

"I stand by the accuracy of that."

"How is your dad?"

"Still not talking to me. Somehow, since the book came out, not talking to me even harder."

"Yeah, Vivian said you wrote a book. What's up with that?"

"Half memoir, half cultural survey, all sexy. At least according to Publisher's Weekly."

"Are you allowed to write half a memoir these days?"

"Oh indeed. One of the girls in my workshop was working on a project that was simultaneously about global warming and how her mother died of lung cancer. It was pretty good."

"But not as sexy as yours."

"Nothing's as sexy as mine."

The engine chose that moment to make an awful choking noise.

·

By the time the engine stopped hacking, dinner was served. The director wanted to talk to Marika about how skin-birds coped with the conditions that drive real birds astray, which led to the question of what was a real animal, anyway, if skins weren't, which led to talk about Marika's book, which led to a short interview on the stern while the sun was setting. Meanwhile, Faith stared at the weather radar, trying to find a pleasing storm to finish off the trip on a potential high note, and talked with Robert, her first mate, about the vacation time he had coming, and worked on the blog, and drank her Laphroig.

Marika disappeared to her bed as soon as the interview was over. It must have been tiring, flying so far.

At breakfast, Faith sat by the director and suggested heading a bit south towards stormier weather, but his budget wouldn't accommodate more than one extra day. Then she checked on the wire-and-duct-tape repairs to the engine -- holding up fine. And then she took a stroll around the lower deck, just to see how things were.

Marika turned out to be inside, talking to Chaz about Indian food. She wrapped that up without seeming to, and followed Faith without seeming to out onto the bow.

"So, I didn't ask you how your dad is doing, yesterday. So rude!" She was still wearing the sunglasses and earrings, but now with a pair of cargo pants and a green t-shirt. Where these changes of clothing came from was a mystery to Faith; it never occurred to her to ask her mother, until it was too late, and Vivian never wanted to talk about it.

She didn't feel ready to ask Marika, either. "He's still speaking to me. More's the pity."

"That implies that you're still speaking to him."

"Now you sound like Dr. Kravitz."

"She was right sometimes."

"It would upset Vivian if I just cut him out of my life."

Marika nodded and pushed her sunglasses up to perch on her head. "Vivian is still making your dad out to be the good guy."

"In her mind it's easy. One person ran away, and it wasn't Dad. Plenty of people agree with her."

"It's the number one question I have to field at readings, you know. Your mom ran out on you. Tell us how mad you are at her, how much it fucked up your life."

"Must make you crazy."

"Nah, I was already crazy, just ask Dr. Kravitz."

"Vivian's getting married soon."

"I believe I may have heard a little something about that, when I stopped by to see her Monday night." Fifteen-year-old Marika would have rolled her eyes, and fifteen-year-old Faith would have been mad at her for it, so maybe they have both grown up a little.

"Her fiance's dad was a bull."

"Heard that, too."

"They have some kind of big plan where instead of her just giving him her skin, they're going to swap."

"Then they're going to hyphenate their names, right?"

Faith sighed. "I just don't see how it's going to be any better. I mean, it is better. He didn't outright steal her skin the way Dad stole Mom's. But she's still going to be trapped."

Marika was silent for a moment, the wind ruffling her earrings. A drop of rain hit the upturned lens of her glasses. "And you ran away to sea."

"That I did."

"Are you looking for your mom?"

"No, Dr. Kravitz. Gannets live in the Atlantic."

"And yet, here you are."

"I just like it out here."

It was raining for real, now, and they retreated inside.

•

After dinner the rain tapered off. Out on deck, Marika leaned carelessly against the rail, and Faith imagined her sunglasses falling off and sinking through the cold water, tumbling, to end up miles below in the silt. Of course they didn't.

As she got closer, she heard Marika muttering.

"...when my dimensions are as well compact, my mind as generous, and my form as true as honest madame's issue?" She turned, and didn't even pretend to be embarrassed by Faith's presence. "One of the few good things about getting locked up in an all-girl boarding school was that we got to play all the boys' roles too."

Faith just looked at her, at the swing of her hair brushing her shoulder, at her earring.

"So I was Edmund in *King Lear*."

Faith nodded. The earring swayed in the breeze.

"You know: Thou, nature, are my goddess..."

"Sounds cool. The only Shakespeare we ever did in high school was *Romeo and Juliet*. I hated it."

"You never had King Lear in college?"

"I mostly took science classes."

Marika chuckled. "All work and no play..."

"The ocean is play. The ocean is beautiful." She wasn't looking at Marika at all now, but she felt the air get warmer and moister in the moment before they kissed.

In the morning, Marika wasn't in Faith's cabin. Her skin was, though, neatly draped over the chair where Faith sat to write her blog posts, the only place in the room where something that size could be neatly draped, impossible to miss.

Faith hesitated for a moment before even picking it up. The feathers were warm, which didn't seem like it should be possible. They left a fine powder on her fingers like butterfly wings.

Marika didn't leave it behind by mistake, that was impossible. She must have wanted Faith to see it, to have the opportunity.

Faith folded it -- her clumsy inexperienced fingers could only get it down to the size of a bath towel -- and took it to Marika's cabin. No one was inside. She put the skin on the bed and locked the door so that no one but Marika would find it. Hook evaded.

Maybe she could ask Vivian for a plus-one for the wedding. It'd be nice to have someone there who understood.

But that was months away. Today, they had to head east.

Carrie Laben is the author of the novel *A Hawk in the Woods* and the forthcoming novella *The Water Is Wide*. Their work has appeared in such venues as *The Dark*, *Electric Literature*, *Indiana Review*, and *Outlook Springs*, winning the Shirley Jackson Award in Short Fiction along the way. They've been a MacDowell Fellow and a resident at the Anne LaBastille Memorial Residency and Brush Creek Foundation for the Arts. They hold an MFA from the University of Montana and live in Queens, where they are at work on their next novel.

a letter to charles white, dated august the second, 1912

s.j. bagley

My dearest Charles,

I am not at all certain this missive shall be welcomed but I felt an explanation needed, such as it is, for my abrupt departure, my 'notable disappearance' as was reported in both the Journal and the wicked rag of the Westerly Sun.

Please, understand, I am not able to make apologies as leaving was the only way to prevent terrible things happening to you and, even now, I can't abide the thought (and I do so miss you, Charles, and the feel of your cock, hard and hot against mine, and the way my throat would feel after being filled with you, the warmth of your bed after we'd both been spent. Such thoughts are as torture to me, here in this cold city I cannot and will not name.)

It all began, if you remember, early last summer. We lunched with your cousin Delores and her dullard of a beau (whose name I shan't ever bother to remember) at that spot near Wood River, the water cold and playful. There were small sandwiches of that Arabian cici bean paste and cucumber, along with that overly sweet overly strong wine that Delores always seemed to have on hand. The sun was high and the air seemed heavy yet somehow frail.

We did our absolute best to appear the paragons of landed machismo but Delores, ever the clever coquette, saw right through it while the dullard, well, he barely seemed to know where he was. The wine flowed like wine and the conversation like scullery gossip and, all told, the afternoon had been quite pleasant if unremarkable.

But, as the trees on the other side of the river began to swallow the sun, the dullard decided to strip and go for a swim, his proud nakedness standing in start contrast to affected naiveté and propriety. After splashing around like some broke-legged swan, he yelled about something sharp and dove down to pull whatever it was from the clay.

Coming out of the water and absolutely flaunting his ridiculous manhood, he had some strange bit of pottery in his hand, which he tried to show us by stumbling forward, tripping, and tossing it right into my lap. He cried out as he fell, a child in a man's body, and I will never forget the sweet malice of your laughter at that moment, the mischief in your eye.

He almost wept as Delores tended to him, his foot streaming blood, thinly, from where he had stepped on the crude piece of fired clay (and it was with such joy that we threw caution to the wind and mocked him, cutting him a dozen times with our wicked tongues).

It was quickly after this that we packed everything up and went back into town, Delores and the dullard going one way while you and I made for your room at the Savoy, marching like soldiers past the doorman and the fop of a concierge (and I still treasure that stony glare he shot us, knowing that we were the height of sexual deviance in that small coastal town and being completely unable to do a blessed thing about it.)

The rest of the day and night were spent, if I recall correctly, deep in the throes of Eros, our wrestling only relenting when one of us needed to take the air or loose our bladder. (And, if I may be coarse for a moment, it still remains the best night that this flesh has endured and you should find solace in the fact that I have, in my strange exile, taken no lovers and, without you, I am chaste as a Quaker!)

Upon waking, the next morning, I found myself alone, you having already left for some sort of tedious meeting with some dreadful accountant or similar such baseborn parasite trying to separate you from your well born fortune. As I lounged, my skin hot against the cool silk of the sheets, I thought of the day before and the dullard's misfortune.

With a sigh, I tossed aside the sheets and walked across the room to my valise, where I had casually stored the artefact from the bottom of the river.

Poring over it, I felt its rough surface, somehow not smoothed by its time in the river, the reddish grey clay of it feeling unsavoury beneath my fingers and I saw that it had some sort of crude painting on it, a hideous thing like some sort of centipede rearing above a group that were little more than stick figures. I tell you, Charles, that, for a brief and impossible moment, it felt not like the sweltering July but the deepest dead of Winter.

I darted back across the room to grab my robe and, safely ensconced, I returned to the thing, equal in my fascination and revulsion.

Why, I must have spent hours staring at it for, all of a sudden, night had fallen and you had returned, your entrance barely registering, as I felt dizzy, my ears gently ringing.

Looking up from it was like being drunk one second and sober the next, a whiplash migraine, and it took a moment to recognise you, not just as you, but even as a person standing in front of me. It took every ounce of will, right then and there, not to throw myself from the window in some sort of horrid ecstasy (and such thoughts of self destruction had never troubled me, before, as I did so enjoy my life of decadence and privilege). Instead, I slipped it into the pocket of my robe, which I then stepped out of, only to disappoint you by saying that I had been struck with a headache, the housewife's old chestnut somehow made more painful for its truth.

It was then that you decided to invite Derby, the terrible artist and worse critic, to come around and take a look at the shard, what with our evening plans being so abruptly cancelled.

Honestly, I can recall so very little of his visit, nor can I recall, in any small part, getting dressed again and going downstairs with you to meet him in the lobby.

As the two of you droned on, bees busy in a hive, I completely ignored you both, pretending to sip some harsh spirit, but you can recall my surprise and disappointment at learning that this wasn't some artefact from the old Narragansett tribe, or any people that were here in this land of plenty before our ancestors settled here but, rather, a contemporary piece by some odd Hungarian.

As Derby, the wretch, continued to drone on about the artist dying in some European war or another, I tossed the whole of my drink down my throat and, without a word to either of you, stepped out and made my way to the canal, to watch the water dance beneath the street lamps.

We argued that morning, the next morning, our last morning. It's funny, really, almost quaint, that I can't recall, at all, what we fought about while I can close my eyes and see every moustache hair, every talon of the delicate crow's feet you were developing, every single thing about how wounded you looked in that moment, how taken aback you were by whatever shallow insult I hurled at you. It haunted me, my love, I swear. It was nigh unbearable for the entire time I was still able to feel something like human emotion. And, even now, some part of me whines in sorrow, begs me to apologise but, honestly, what would it even mean?

We both dressed quickly, you declaring that you would be going back to your uncle's house for a while, letting me stay in the hotel room, alone, as a feeble punishment. We broke our fast quickly, the eggs runny and the bacon burnt.

I saw it in your eyes when you left, the fear. Not of losing me in some inane argument but of something neither of us could comprehend. I had already begun to change, Charles, and I can't know how much you saw, whether you saw that I had begun to sweat constantly, that I had so rapidly begun to smell like sourdough (so appealing in the proper context and so awful, otherwise.)

I was already... not me. But nor was I yet to become me, or, to be more honest, I was in but the first instar of my new life.

Later that morning, I found myself with the shard of pottery again in my hand. I had been placing the edge of it under my fingernails, sweeping it from side to side as if obsessively cleaning beneath them with it. Lord knows how long i had been at it before I noticed that the nails had begun to loosen from their beds, the soft flesh below gently pulped by the sharp clay, yet entirely bloodless.

In a panic, I jumped from my chair, grabbed my black suede gloves, finished dressing, and stepped out into the early afternoon, strolling through downtown Westerly and through Wilcox Park, the shard safely tucked in my jacket pocket where it felt impossibly heavy.

As I walked, doing my level best to appear normal (and completely failing) and tipping my hat to the locals that would pale upon seeing me, asking each other in hushed tones if I was alright, if they should fetch help. As this continued and I found their shifty gazes intolerable, I lurched into the library, almost tumbling down the stairs on my way to the rare books room.

Charles, I cannot truly express how strange and out of sorts I felt, how so much of the day seemed blurry, sticky around the edges, as I tore through the collection of rare occult books that stood in a locked bookcase (and I have no recollection of smashing the lock and tearing the door off, but there it was) looking for... something, some book that I somehow knew held the next piece to the puzzle of my Grand Becoming.

Finally, I found it, a book in what looked like some sort of crude Italian with the margins filled with such tiny and cramped script that it was almost illegible and I had to hold it directly beneath the gas lamp to read it, my whole being growing simultaneously nausated and somehow... centered.

(Of the words written in that horrid and beautiful Bible i can only remember bits and bobs, the rest just existing as... impressions, but you will find it in a safe deposit box, 2342, in the Washington Trust bank right across from the library. The smaller of the two keys I have enclosed in this envelope will open it. You must get it, Charles, and you must read it, you must understand it.)

After some time had passed, my ability to judge impaired, I stuck the book in my pocket, feeling it grow oddly and comfortingly warm as it nestled against the shard, and I ran back up the stairs, knocking the matron aside on my way out, and I continued to run, her shouts fading in the background, back to the hotel room where I quickly packed and then waited in the lobby, having had the concierge call for a carriage to take me to you.

But, as you know, I never arrived. As I waited, I took the book back out and began to read parts of it, again, seeing that some of the scribbles were quite recent and that they spoke of something called The Queen of Cats (which had been referenced extensively under different names and slightly different descriptions all through the text.)

I knew, then and there, that this was the thing marked on the shard that the dullard so haplessly discovered, the shard that would forever change me and, I so dearly hope, will change you. I knew then that Derby's Hungarian artist wasn't simply one of any number of foolish European men, dabbling in art and craft while waiting between wars but, rather, was something of a prophet. Someone who had not just known of this Queen of Cats but who somehow had intimate knowledge of her, and a more intimate understanding of her.

I read a bit further while still awaiting the sluggish carriage, whose driver would certainly find some way to bilk me for his time, reading about a house that, with a shock, I immediately recognised, for we had passed it, so many times, traveling between Westerly and your uncle's house in Shannock.

It was then that the carriage finally arrived and I jumped into it, throwing some coins at the driver, shouting to him to take me to you as quickly as possible.

Again, however, I never made it there.

As we came upon the house, that pale blue saltbox, all sunbleach and dry rot, ageworn and somehow so breathlessly uncanny as if it simply didn't belong, couldn't belong, to any place on this Earth. A house we had seen, often, when traveling past that awful little hamlet of Bradford on our way to your uncle's house in Shannock. A house that you had often referred to as an eyesore but, not once, did we really think of it beyond that and how strange is that? This impossible place, this shrine to something no sane person would term a 'God,' was right beneath your gently upturned nose but we just couldn't see it for what it was, as if we were not ALLOWED to truly see it and around it were hundreds of cats, all facing it, their heads pressed down against the barren soil as if in prayer to some hideous corruption of that most beautiful Mecca.

I positively screamed at the driver to stop, to let me out, to abandon me. And he did, his horses running back toward civilisation as if their lives depended on it.

I grew dizzy, falling forward, my ears filled with cotton, my limbs filled with lead.

I came to, bolting upright, inside the house.

(I still have no idea how I had entered, whether of my own free will in some strange fugue or whether taken inside by someone or something else, but, I suppose, that doesn't matter.)

I was in the front room, the fading afternoon light showing that the house seemed to be entirely empty of furniture, its walls papered over with old newspapers in no discernible order, yellow as jaundice with age.

I stood, shakily, and walked toward the back of the house, seeing a lantern next to one of the two bedrooms, both of which had no doors, just gaping darkness.

I lit the lantern and steadied myself, catching my breath, the remaining dizziness leaving me while I found myself, once again, drenched in sweat, not of nerves but just of... being. As I imagine the fish, the frogs, to be.

I walked through the door of the left-hand room and

froze as the light shewed me something that, only two days prior would have left me screaming in terror and running from that place.

There were bodies, children's bodies, stacked like cordwood, mummified, covered with something like spider silk but pale yellow and reeking of something like root vegetables gone off and left to rot. I counted a dozen before I stopped, too horrified to continue, and backed out of the room, jumping at a sound from up the rickety stairs, something shifting in the loft.

I began to climb the stairs, one hand on the railing the other gripping the lantern tightly in my gloved fist, knowing that what I should be doing is leaving, somehow finding the authorities and making them aware of the nightmare in the room below.

But I kept climbing, any notions of terror and horror subdued by some indescribable anticipation at which, I am not ashamed to say, I grew as hard as I ever did in your gentle hands, your soft mouth.

What greeted me at the top of the stairs, in the loft just outside the last bedroom, was a convocation of cats, clearly those that I had seen swearing their supplication outside, all sat in neat geometric rows, their eyes shining in the pale lamplight, gazing at me with what I now know was affection.

Carefully, so as not to tread on any of my feline audience, I crept toward the door, a heavy oak thing, roughly hewn and hardwared with dull cast iron, which I fully expected to be near impossible to open but it swung open soundlessly at the most gentle of touches.

Taking a deep breath, I hesitated, looking around at all of the cats staring at me, their bodies vibrating with a low, almost imperceptible, purr, all in harmony.

I went in.

In the room lay a carpet of leaves, an autumn's forest worth, of every local kind imaginable, coming close to my knees at its highest, and at the center of which was a large marble slab, raw and unworked, but still shining in the light that seemed to somehow grow brighter.

I am not sure how to explain or truly describe it (or even if there could be any real earthly explanation) but that thing, that Queen of Cats, was, as I had suspected, so clearly the same thing crudely painted on that bit of pottery from the river, from that last good day, and I could not help but think that all of it, from Delores' dullard's distasteful dive into the river until this very moment of me writing to you, before I return to Her tonight, my pockets full of teeth and bone, has been entirely out of our control and, rather, some sort of plan put in place long before we lunched on a lazy summer day.

Long before we even were, Charles.

You see, she is a 'cat' in the most abstract notion, a vaguely feline vermiform covered in pale orange and dirty white fur, whiskers like the wriggling tendrils of some grotesque anemone, dozens of small misshapen limbs sticking out from her sides at seemingly random places, her mouth like some sort of puckered anus (and I do hope you'll forgive the vulgarity but I cannot think of a better way to describe it,) and her eyes, Charles, her awful eyes, a dozen or so scattered around the top of her earless head, each one crusted and rheumy like that horrid old Portugese fellow we would see at the park, each one boring into me.

What happened next, my darling Charles, I will never be allowed to know. I only recall waking in a strange bed, in a strange town, in a strange land, filled with strange people.

The years between then and now have been filled with Good Works I am not at liberty to write down but, I promise, I will tell you everything when you join me.

Ten years, I know, is a long time, but I have kept eyes upon you and I know that you still pine for me, for our Arcadia, just as I know you cannot refute this summons.

Come, as soon as you can, to that pale blue saltbox, on the road between your uncle's house in Shannock and Westerly.

Come.

And let me be as clear as I can, Charles. I go to Her, tonight, not to engage in some absurd act of heroism, not to attempt to end Her, but to pledge myself to her, to kneel in exaltation, my head upon the soil, her thoughts like a kitten's purr in the back of my everything.

Come and listen.

yrs. with love and longing,
David Bussey.

s.j. bagley is a multidisciplinary artist, philosopher, poet, and weirdo what edits and publishes THINKING HORROR: A JOURNAL OF HORROR PHILOSOPHY and the irregularly published zine/journal/thing SOFT TEETH (and, occasionally, does other things).

they live with a cat, a dog, and many centipedes in the woods, near the ocean, at the bottom of new england.

But Only Because I Love You

Molly Tanzer

The sky above is impossibly blue, striped with bright bands of clouds tinged pink and orange with the coming sunrise. There are a few stars still sparkling in the heavens, and the moon, bigger than it looks beyond the borders of this land, hangs low and near.

The pack of spotted jackals is also near. Their baying is a goad. If we do not find some shelter, some escape, we are done for. The wind whips our scent into their long noses, maddening them. They will tear us to pieces if they catch us.

I am not worried. I have no reason to be. Not yet.

We are all gasping as we run up the side of a low hillock, even me, long used to ascents. I am weighted down with most of our gear and our water reserve, and that, I am less used to, though the last month has hardened me considerably.

"Come on, Bridget!" shouts Dr. Sangare, pelting pell-mell down the side of the hill, nearly slipping on the waving grasses. One hand keeps her tattered, dusty bowler in place against the gusts, the other windmills her back into balance as her pack slams hard on her hip. Her tweed jacket flies open, revealing the knives strapped across her chest. She is good with them, but not good enough to stop a pack of ravenous dogs from rending us limb from limb. "We must get to that...thingy!"

The thingy is a rocky prominence in the distance. If we were closer to home, I would think it was a cairn to mark the path for travelers. But we are not close to home, and here there are no marked paths. Or travelers, for that matter.

"I don't think," gasps Bridget, "we'll make it." She is struggling too, nearly tripping as her skirts whip and snap around her ankles like a prayer flag. The leather and bronze hip holster glimmers bright as her flaming hair; she is an excellent shot but the dogs are too many, too quick to make her superb marksmanship useful.

"We must make it," says Dr. Sangare. Her fierce determination steadies Bridget. They are a good team, they complement one another.

Neither calls to me. Why should they? I have proven myself strong and reliable time and again, and besides, I cannot return their encouragement. Anyway, I was not hired to cheer them onward. I was hired to carry into Leng what they could not manage by themselves, and haul back what they raided from the barrows of her ancient queens.

As we keep running, the spire in the distance takes on new details. To my surprise, it does appear to be a cairn—but an enormous one. Vaguely pyramidal in shape, wind and rain has smoothed away the rougher edges of the piled boulders; some have tumbled from the heights and lie scattered about the base.

"It's too far." Bridget is lagging behind her companion, I can see her legs are shaking with fatigue. "Dily... I... I don't think we'll be dying rich."

"What's our plan once we're there?"

Dr. Sangare's question distracts Bridget from her worries; she is already assessing the tactical possibilities, and runs the faster for it. "To the top," she says. "High ground. We'll each take up a station, pick off as many as we can with boulders, rocks, my pistol, whatever we can find. Maybe if we keep them at bay for long enough they'll get bored."

"All right," says Dr. Sangare. Sweat gleams on her dark forehead, it glistens like stars against the night sky. "Got that, Krishna?"

She looks back. I nod.

"He's smiling," observes Bridget, as we redouble our pace. "The fuck is he smiling about? Doesn't he know we're in danger?"

"Try asking him," says Dr. Sangare.

"Right," says Bridget.

If I could, I would tell them that we are in danger... but not in danger of dying. I would know. But I cannot tell them, so I do not, and we run on in silence.

Though they carry less than I, they have more trouble than I climbing up the slippery rocks when we reach them. Well, neither grew up trekking from village to village over dangerous passes, or scrambling up escarpments to get at berries or birds' eggs.

As the jackals bound closer, a slavering yipping howling mass of furry, toothy hunger, Bridget slips a second time. I sling off my pack and go down to help her up.

"Thanks, Krishna," she wheezes, as she clambers up beside me, now marginally safer.

Unlike many visitors to my home village, Bridget and Dr. Sangare have always been polite. I nod in response to her thanks, and shouldering the pack, I point higher.

Dr. Sangare has gotten above us, squatting on the top of the rock pile. The sun has risen, and she tips up the brim of her bowler, squinting in the dawn light.

"There's an awful lot of them," she observes.

"We'll do what we can. I mean, we've made it this far." Bridget hauls herself onto a flattish boulder and sets to looking over her pistol. "Krishna, anything to add?"

I shrug.

"Even facing down death, still silent as the grave?" Bridget shakes her head. The handful of ruddy curls that have escaped her tight bun bounce.

"Here they come," says Dr. Sangare. Her black eyes glint as she raises a boulder the size of my head over her own. Hurling it down upon the jackals, it bounces once, twice, then strikes one in the face. Its jaw is torn off and the resulting red spray mists those next to it. The jawless jackal runs another step, then falls over twitching.

The dead jackal's companions pause for a moment to look at the ruined corpse of their companion, then turn to look at us. One growls.

"Woo!" cries Dr. Sangare, pointing at the dogs. "That's right, you mangy mongrels!"

Dr. Sangare turns around, looking this way and that for another rock. She spies a candidate, resting at the meeting point of two large boulders. She steps out onto the flatter, lower of the two. It wobbles beneath her foot, and tips inward.

"Dily!" cries Bridget, leaping to her partner's side, but the doctor is already sliding, slipping into the black chasm. She screams, once, and then we hear a terrible thump.

Bridget is there, kneeling, peering down, calling Dr. Sangare's name. There is no response. I peek over the edge; it's impossible to see anything.

A growl turns my attention behind me. Three jackals have gained the top of the mound. One barks. Another snarls. I think about what color the snarl might have been, in my mind, before my color-sense changed. Before I could only see one color in my mind. One color that meant one thing.

They advance. I make my decision.

I push Bridget into the blackness. She screams as I jump in after. But of course, I do not make a sound as I fall.

•

I used to hear in color, and count and smell, too. The sound of Mother patting out parathas was warm golden yellow, the smell of our yak a fresh green; a pile of five stones was maroon, but a pile of seven, pale purple. I didn't see these colors, not exactly... Zopa, our yak, was creamy white and warm brown, and stones were... stone colored. Just the same, I knew the colors were there, hovering at the edges of my understanding of the world, but vital to it. When I thought hard about certain things, I could sense the color with it in my mind. It was never distracting; in fact, it often helped me remember things, like how many sheepskins I'd last seen in the barn.

All that changed when I went to see where the star struck near the base of Chomolungma, Mother of the World, which visitors call Mount Everest. The night before, we all had seen it streaking through the sky, its tail redder than the War God's skin. Everyone was curious, of course, but some people in our village refused to go see what had fallen—the oldtimers in particular said that if it had been cast out of Heaven, it was not for man to look upon. Those of us who would go went anyways, laughing at them, and at their children, sour-faced and resentful at being kept at home.

The crater was smoking like a cup of su cha on a cold morning when we came upon it, but in spite of all the dead trees and blackened stones the earth was not too warm to walk on. Still, the strangeness of it put off many of our party, and they stood well away from the lip of the depression.

Something did seem wrong... it was the shadows, as if the sun shone differently upon that place than elsewhere. My sister begged me not to go nearer, and many agreed we should turn around. I would not listen, and went to see, walking over the hot earth until at last I saw what lay at the center. It was a rough, vaguely spherical stone not much smaller than a wagon-wheel. I approached the steaming boulder, and saw a long fissure ran along it.

I am not sure what I thought I might see if I gazed into its depths, but gaze I did. What lurked within was of such a strange nature! I would call it a color... but it was not a color I knew.

No one else looked within, in part because I am told once I saw this sight I uttered a wordless cry and staggered back before collapsing. And the next day, when others from our village went to inspect the place, the object, and whatever had lurked within it, had unaccountably disappeared.

This was all told to me afterwards; I lay unconscious for nearly a week. And when I awoke, I found that either I or the world had changed. Whatever it was, color or some-thing else, I had been blinded by it, in part. I still saw, but from that day forth I no longer felt the blue-green comfort of the number nine, or knew the crimson warmth of the sound of cattle lowing.

It had also taken my voice from me. I could not say a word after waking from that strange, dreamless slumber. Before I got used to silence, I would try, only to become so overwhelmed with the memory of what I had seen that it seemed to me the world spun faster under my feet, and I was in danger of falling off it. I quickly trained myself to not speak—or think about speaking, and not long after that, I found I would rather keep silent...for I discovered that see-ing what I had seen had not only taken something from me, but given me something in return.

I first noticed it when grandmother passed me my plate of dal bhat one night. Her hand shook in a strange way, spilling the hot lentils on my lap. Later, when I was resentfully scrubbing out my chhuba, I thought about her, and how the color, that color, had infused the memory, clinging to her as a butterfly clings to a flower in a stiff wind. I did not understand the significance, but as long as I thought of her, the color was there.

A day later, a spasm shook her. She messed herself, and then she started making a sound halfway between a groan and a cry. There was nothing anyone could do. She wailed and grunted all night. When the dawn broke, she finally stopped, but it was because she had died.

For a time, I worried I had killed her. I carried the weight of it like a faggot of wood until I saw the color again, in my mind, when my father's brother by marriage went to another village to trade, and stayed away longer than expected. A day later, a party was sent out to find him, only to discover he had been crushed beneath a falling tree while camping for the night. It was not clear when the accident had occurred, but I thought it unlikely I had caused it.

Just the same, I felt no relief, for I knew then the awful truth about what it meant to see that color in my mind. It was a terrible thing, and I felt I would almost rather die than live among those I loved, knowing when they must die.

When Dr. Sangare and Bridget arrived in our village, asking for a guide to Leng, it surprised my family when I volunteered to escort the two strange women to that dangerous land from whence few ever returned. I helped them to understand as best I could that I wanted to go—made the point that my knowledge of English would be a boon to their little expedition. In the end, they accepted my gestured explanations, and let me go, though reluctantly.

For the first time since I was struck dumb I was grateful that I could not communicate the truth. How could I explain that I would rather focus my attention on those whom I did not care if they died?

·

The expedition started off well enough. Dr. Sangare and Bridget were excellent travelers, willing to wake up early, help fix meals, and best of all, they kept to a reasonable pace and therefore never suffered from the altitude or the distance. They had packed more than necessary, but everyone always does; I knew that from hearing my cousins talk about guiding hikers. But my companions hadn't taken all that much more than they needed, and they always carried some of their own gear.

They were kind and friendly, always making sure I was eating and drinking enough, and never making fun of me when they did something I found bizarre, or vice versa. I knew that trekkers were often rude to their guides, so I felt lucky. It made the journey much more enjoyable than I expected.

They knew about me only what the other English-speakers in my village had told them—that I had learned English from a monk who had come to our monastery all the way from Kathmandu, that I had often trekked through the Himalayas, and knew the pass that would take them through to Leng. They told me similarly little of themselves, but I put together a kind of history from their conversations, so I knew that Dr. Sangare had traveled to England from a country called Mali in order to study medicine. But, as women were not allowed at the university, she had learned to dress and act like an Englishman in order to earn her degree, and liked it so much she retained her suits even after she left.

Or rather, was asked to leave. After only a year. Pretending to be a man had gotten her in the door, but she could not pretend away the color of her skin. The other students had made life difficult for her, stealing her books, humiliating her in class, preventing her from accessing the various laboratories open to the student doctors. In order to get enough experience in dissecting corpses she'd ended up needing to exhume her own. When she was caught, instead of seeing her dedication for what it was, her college had shown her the door. Dr. Sangare was of the opinion they'd been only too glad to see the back of her; almost grateful to her for giving them a reason to do so, so early in her career.

Bridget was possessed of as checkered a past. She had had many trades, most of them involving some degree of law-breaking, and was possessed of many skills, the majority of them illegal. She was a survivor, cunning and wise, but kind and cheerful too.

Dr. Sangare had opened an unlicensed women's clinic after being dismissed, helping working women with illnesses picked up in any number of common ways, as well as providing family planning services. It was there that she'd met Bridget, and while one was dark and the other fair, one educated and one world-wise, each had seen herself in the other.

The capital Dr. Sangare used to open her clinic had come largely from the sale of certain personal effects she had claimed from those bodies she had procured while still in medical school. Unfortunately, given her chosen clientele's lack of solvency, she didn't make enough to keep herself in medicine and meals, and also bribe the lawmakers into looking the other way when they realized what she was doing.

Bridget stuck by Dr. Sangare even after the scandal, offering her a place to stay when her clinic was shut down and her assets were all seized. While living together they discussed the sensational news regarding a Dr. Carter's recent expedition to Egypt—as well as the estimated value of what he had discovered. Dr. Sangare knew how to rob a grave, and Bridget knew how to get by on not a lot, even in unfamiliar places, so they decided almost that very night to try something similar. The pockets of the unwary and the graves of the damned supplied everything they needed to get to someplace with deeper pockets and more fabulous graves. And in order to make the most from their efforts, they decided that they would keep the expedition to just the two of them.

How they settled on Leng I never did find out. All I heard was that they had "obtained" a map allegedly showing the burial valley of Leng's ancient warrior queens; after we made it over the pass, it was toward this we headed. I was never as convinced of its existence as they were, but I hoped it was real. Though I was appalled by Dr. Sangare's grave-robbing, and alarmed by Bridget's nonchalance about having been a hired killer, thief, and prostitute at various times in her life, I came to respect them both for their determination and passion. I came to like them.

I like to think they came to respect me and like me, too.

•

I awaken, tasting dirt and blood. I spit out a tooth, which bounces away and disappears. It is black down in the pit; I see nothing but a patch of sky through the hole we tumbled through.

I feel around in the darkness, and cut myself before discovering our lantern, shattered in the fall. Were I able, I'd curse, for the hot gush between my thumb and forefinger makes me aware of the sticky blood on my face, in my eyes; the scrapes all over my body.

I find some bit of ragged cloth and wrap my hand, which makes it easier to get one of our emergency candles lit. The brightness sets my eyes watering, but eventually I can see enough to look around.

We are in a conical cave. Cobwebs cling to everything, and the floor is littered with dusty chunks of masonry. The most interesting thing is the staircase, spiraling to the hole above along the side of the structure. I frown at it, as I feel my aches and pains from the fall.

My two companions are slumped on the floor. I trot over to them. They are both breathing, but Bridget's arm is twisted under her body in a way that sets my stomach rolling. She will need medical attention. Fortunately, there's a doctor close at hand.

I drizzle some of our precious water onto Dr. Sangare's face, getting a little in her mouth. She sputters and licks her lips, then gingerly pushes herself to a seated position.

"Krishna!" She looks around. "Are we safe?"

I nod.

"How did you get down here?"

I point skyward.

"You jumped?" She seems annoyed. "Now we're all stuck!"

I point at the stairs. Her eyes widen.

"You knew?"

I shook my head.

"What a damn fool thing to do!"

I raise an eyebrow, folding my arms over my chest. She sighs.

"What I mean is thank you." She winces, stretching out her legs. The knee of her trouser has been ripped away, and her black flesh beneath is red and pink with blood. "At the very least we're safe from those jackals in here."

I point at Bridget. Dr. Sangare gasps, and pulls herself over to her partner.

"She's still out cold! We need to get her up."

I pour water into Bridget's mouth. She does not stir.

Dr. Sangare frowns. She looks worried. I am not. If Bridget were in real danger, I'd know.

"Bridget!" She shakes the girl. "Come on!"

"Gngh," says Bridget, eyelids flickering. "Ow."

We get her up, and take a look at her arm. It is definitely broken.

"We'll have to set it," Dr. Sangare says, frown deepening.

I can see how much pain Bridget is in already, and hold

up a single finger. While they watch, mystified, I pack a chillum with hash. I pantomime how to smoke.

"What..." Bridget winces. "I suppose I can't ask why."

I consider this and point to my arm, making a wracked expression, as if I'm in pain.

"I see." She looks to Dr. Sangare, who shrugs. "Well, I suppose I'll try it..."

I help her get the pipe lit off the candle, and encourage her as she hacks and coughs on the thick smoke. When we see the relaxation on her face, we know it's time.

Dr. Sangare puts her belt between Bridget's teeth, a wise precaution. It is my job to hold her as Dr. Sangare sets the bone. She screams, but recovers quickly, as Dr. Sangare splints the arm and then constructs a makeshift sling from a scarf. When she's finished, I pass out some goat jerky.

"Well, that's done," mumbles Bridget, through a mouthful, "but even if the jackals are gone, I'm afraid I'll need to rest a bit."

"I suppose I'll do some exploring," says Dr. Sangare, finishing her portion with one enormous bite. "This place must have been made by people for some purpose. Let's see if they left anything behind."

She grabs a piece of firewood and makes a torch of it, tearing Bridget's petticoat into strips to wrap around one end and dousing it all in the last of our lamp oil. Bridget giggles, watching this, but I make the concerned Dr. Sangare understand that this is normal, a side effect of the hash.

Dr. Sangare begins to wave her torch about. We see there is a cavernous door in the wall; a corridor that slopes downward. We must be beneath ground level, but we can go yet deeper.

She looks from the door to me. "Krishna—want to come?"

I look from Dr. Sangare to Bridget. The girl nods.

"I'll be fine," she says vaguely, helping herself to more jerky.

Before I go, I wrap the remainder and tuck it out of sight. If the hunger comes on her, as it can with hash sometimes, I don't want her eating everything we have left.

The ceiling is much lower in the tunnel. Dr. Sangare and I pad along, her hunched over; me upright with my head only a few inches from the rock, winding our way deeper as we go. Our path is a spiral, curving in on itself, a continuation of the staircase leading out of the conical chamber above. I see Dr. Sangare checking her pocket watch every so often. She's timing our descent. It occurs to me that this is a woman used to sneaking around in unfamiliar places.

In unfamiliar graves.

"I wonder what this place is," she mutters. "It wasn't on our map..."

I cannot muse with her, but having looked at that map, which had only the vaguest markings, I am hardly surprised it left a few things off.

Eventually the tunnel bottoms out. A low gate has been built into the living rock, two stone slabs topped with a third. There is a chamber beyond the portal, and Dr. Sangare immediately squats down, thrusting the torch within and peering about.

I am more concerned by the hideous carving of a jackal-headed monster that sits atop the portal. Wings curve from its shoulder blades and teeth from its maw. It is hideous, sinister, and Dr. Sangare's torchlight glints off the polished stones of its eyes in a way that makes it look almost alive.

I find it strange that no door blocks our passage. There is only this silent stone guardian protecting what lies within. I note there is some kind of writing carved at its cruel feet.

"Coming?" asks Dr. Sangare. She seems excited.

I point to the statue; the unfamiliar script. Dr. Sangare shrugs impatiently.

"There's gold in there," she says, and darts inside.

I consider whether I will go in after her, and that's when I see it. The color. Like the halo of flames surrounding the glorious goddess Palden Lhamo, the color is all around Dr. Sangare in my mind's eye. I cannot say anything, and when I think about trying the blackness appears behind my eyes with that telltale sensation of faintness.

Something about this place has doomed her. She does not know it, but I do.

I dart inside after her. Perhaps it isn't too late.

Once I'm through, I can't think of the color in my mind, for I am overwhelmed with all the very real gold. It limns the cave and every object in it, red-gold and yellow-gold and orange-gold, depending on where Dr. Sangare's torch is burning. She is running to and fro, staring at everything, mouth open.

"Krishna!" she calls. Her voice is pitched higher than usual. "This is it! Look at it all!"

I am looking. Heaps of coins, diadems, bangles, cloth of cold, gold and jewel-encrusted weapons, even mirrors, the golden backing riming the reflective glass like early ice along the edges of a frozen puddle. It is a queen's barrow, such as my companions dreamed of finding.

Dr. Sangare whoops and sings, racing from one pile to the next, selecting baubles and shoving handfuls of coins in her pockets. I sit back, dismayed, wondering what here could spell her doom. Is there a trap? A curse? Everything and nothing seems possible in that glimmering grave.

She slings a heavy chain of gold links around my neck before I can stop her. "Very handsome!" she hoots, before going deeper to see what else she can see.

I am still squatting near the entrance when I hear, "Krishna!" I lope quickly after her, worried, but when I find her amid the splendor I see that she is excited, not upset. She has found the queen—or at least a queenly-looking skeleton, perched upon a throne. She holds a sword in one hand, and some sort of idol in the other. The weight of a heavy crown has caused her clean white skull to list forward.

The crown comes to two strange points. They look like long ears.

"I want it." Dr. Sangare is transfixed not by the crown or the sword but by the golden object clutched in the queen's left hand. It is a miniature version of the guardian I saw above the tomb's entrance. "Hold this," she says, thrusting the torch into my hands.

The color in my mind is brighter than ever, and I realize the idol is the source of the danger. I pluck at her tweed sleeve, urging her to leave it be, come away.

"What?" she asks, annoyed.

I point at the statuette and shake my head. She rolls her eyes. I tighten my grasp on her wrist. I shake my head again. I wish I could tell her something, anything, but I cannot, so I do not.

"Don't be so superstitious," she snaps, wresting herself free.

I step back. I have never heard a tone like that in her voice. It frightens me. I point at it, and her, but I know not how to tell her without words that the gilded thing means death.

"I didn't hire you to lecture me," she says, turning back to the idol. She lifts it gingerly enough, but the skeleton comes unbalanced once the weight is gone and falls forward with a rattle of dry bones. The head bows, the sword clatters to the ground in a puff of dust, and the free hand jerks forward.

A finger points directly at Dr. Sangare.

She takes no notice; she is too entranced by her find, the tiny model of a winged snarling jackal now cradled in her hands. She leans in to the torchlight, studying its intricate details.

"Bridget," she breathes, "oh, Bridget... don't you worry. We'll die rich, yes we fucking will."

I resist the urge to knock it out of her hands, cast the thing away. What good would it do? She is resolved upon having it, was resolved before she even picked it up. I see it in her eyes, and in her posture. The way she touches it.

"Just think of what the British Museum will pay for it." She grins at me. "Eat your heart out, Lawrence of Arabia! Dily of Leng is about to eclipse your fame!"

I carry an armful of riches back up the spiraling corridor, but my heart is heavier than the gold. I can share none of their joy over the find, though I know it is extraordinary. They do not notice my mood. They are too busy delighting in their fortune. Dr. Sangare shows it all to Bridget, piece by piece. I notice she gives every item to her partner to fondle, save for the idol. That, she holds before Bridget's eyes, keeping it in her own hands.

"How much can we carry back, is the question?"

Bridget and Dr. Sangare look over at me.

"Krishna, what do you think?"

What I think and what I can communicate are two very different things. I look at their gear, and think about the volume of gold below our feet. Assuming they are willing to leave behind everything that is not essential to our survival, I imagine I can carry back quite a bit of splendid treasure.

In order to get this across, I rummage through a bag. I find Dr. Sangare's favorite teacup and Bridget's two spare corsets. I show them to my companions, mystifying them, and then set them away from the pile of gold. I point to one, then the other, and shake my head.

"We'll have to downsize." Bridget gets it first. "Of course! I can help with that, while you and Dily pick out the choicest keepsakes." She sighs. "I see now why expeditions always have a dozen or more people, camels, horses, carts... too bad we couldn't afford all that, eh Dily?"

"Next time," she says.

Dr. Sangare and I spend the next few hours down in the queen's vault. I do not fail to notice the bulge in her coat pocket as she sifts through the treasure. She did not leave the idol above; it is with her, with us, in the cave. I wonder if she put it down if the color would retreat from my mind, but I have little hope of this. Dr. Sangare's hand finds the object often, checking to make sure it is there as she selects other items of varying size and varying value.

I am flattered by how strong she must think me, but eventually I must protest, when the pile grows to unreasonable proportions.

"What?"

I make a motion that I hope conveys my desire that she stop. She gets it after a moment, and sighs.

"All right," she says wistfully. "But I can carry some too, you know."

I glance at the heap of treasure. It is more than three men could carry comfortably, and while Dr. Sangare is strong, Bridget has never been particularly robust, and now she has a broken arm. But, I know it will be easier to object when she realizes she may risk tearing the canvas of our pack and taking nothing back at all.

Even with her broken arm, Bridget has not been idle. She has significantly reduced their gear. I return a few crucial items, and then set to loading our spoils.

"Let's eat and go," says Dr. Sangare, eyeing the stairs and the patch of light above. "I want to be out of this hole."

"All right," says Bridget. "I suppose there's no advantage to waiting around."

There is, but I cannot explain they should sleep, that both look vaguely maniacal after all the excitement. I just pack, and pack, and pack, occasionally checking the weight and then packing more.

When I feel I have loaded the bag sufficiently, I alert my companions. Bridget has been dozing, but Dr. Sangare is awake, staring at the winged jackal, watching it as if it might fly away at any moment.

"No room at the inn?" asks Dr. Sangare, pointing at the remainder.

I have no idea what she means, not really, but I shake my head.

"Ah well, it can't be helped," she says, hefting the bag. Her eyes widen. "You've packed it so heavy I'll be amazed if you can make it down from here, much less carry it back to some place where we can hire a cart. You sure this is all right?"

I nod.

"You never fail to impress, Krishna," she says.

I smile, but it feels strained. The color is still around her, and I cannot feel like a triumphant adventurer with that hanging over me.

I follow Dr. Sangare and Bridget up the curving steps to the top of the cave. They are in a fabulous mood, and agree there is no way the jackals will have lingered as long as we were unconscious. I have no idea how long we were really out, but I too hope it was long enough for the pack to lose interest and hunt some other game.

It appears so. We are the only living things to be seen on that windswept, forgotten plateau when we emerge, save for a few bees buzzing in the tall grasses.

"Can I help you? Do you need help getting down?" Dr. Sangare is already halfway down from the top of the rock spire, but Bridget remains with me. "I know I only have one arm, but..."

I smile; shake my head no. I am touched that in her condition she would think of me, but I am more worried for her than for myself.

She takes it slow, and is able to clamber down without incident. Afternoon fades to evening as we descend.

Dr. Sangare waits for us near the bottom, sitting cross-legged on a boulder.

"All right!" she says brightly. "Time to go home!"

I step off the rock. My feet sink into the springy turf, going deeper than normal due to the weight on my back.

"Home," says Bridget. "Fancy that. And far sooner than we expected!"

I help her down beside me, and she favors me with a smile.

"I like this buttered cha we've been getting," says Dr. Sangare as she jumps down beside us, "but a cup of builder's tea sounds like—"

A distant rumble as her feet touch the ground stills her tongue. At first I think it is thunder, but then the rumbling grows louder, and louder, and the rock spire begins to shake. I back away quickly, and my companions follow me as the structure collapses in on itself with a tremendous roar of stone pounding stone; earth falling onto earth.

We watch in shock, getting dust and dirt in our open mouths. When it is over, Dr. Sangare spits, rubs her eyes and whistles.

"Glad we took so much with us," she says.

Bridget gawps at her. "We almost died," she exclaims.

"I thought you didn't want to die poor." Dr. Sangare grins at her.

"No, but—"

This time, it is a howl that interrupts their banter. It appears we are not the only ones who noticed the disturbance on the plateau.

"Where are they?" asks Bridget, glancing about. "Where's it coming from?"

Dr. Sangare looks to me, as if I might have an answer. I shrug. The wind makes it difficult to tell. We wait, tense, and watch.

The first black shape on the horizon answers the question. Bridget spies them first, points. Dr. Sangare draws her knives.

"You want to make a stand?" she asks.

"Where can we run?" is Dr. Sangare's answer. I see her point, dump my pack, and draw my khukuri. Bridget already has her pistol in hand.

It seems like there are more of them than before as they bound closer to us, their shadows long in the fading light. The jackals fan out and surround us, circling us as we stand back to back, the pack with all our loot at the center of our triad. They snarl and growl and snap, some even dart in momentarily to see if we will break and allow ourselves to be swarmed. I am frightened for the first time, for I never can tell when a person will die once the color touches them, and I do not know whether my talent extends to myself. Bridget seems safe, for now, so perhaps this is not the end for us. I cannot imagine how she alone would escape.

The dogs circle us. Up close, I see their pelts are ragged; their bones show through the skin. Starvation makes them vicious.

"Flea-bitten mutts," hisses Dr. Sangare. "Come closer, I dare you!"

"They have no reason to keep back," says Bridget. "They're waiting for something."

"They're waiting for us to flinch," says Dr. Sangare. "They want an opening."

"Do we give them what they want?"

"I think it's time. I'll fire a shot into one, see what they do."

I clutch my khukuri a little tighter as the report echoes across the plateau. A howl is cut short, and then they mob us.

My khukuri is sharp, and I know how to use it. I slice downwards across the throat of the first jackal that springs at me, and the blade glints red in the last of the light. As the jackal falls dead, another leaps; I kick the first away and raise my knife again, this time chopping straight down through the skull of the beast.

As I jerk the blade out of its brains, two come at me. I drop low, use the pommel to stick one in the eye and then bring it back around to stab the other. I get it in the side, and it takes a second strike to finish it off. By the time I'm done the first has bitten me on the calf and is worrying at the meat there. I keep my head and stab it in the side of the neck. Its jaws tighten as it dies, and I fall back, coming down hard on my ass as the beast shits itself in its death throes.

I crane my neck see how my companions fare. Bridget has felled a pile of them with her pistol but is now frantically trying to reload in the twilight, standing behind Dr. Sangare, who is holding her own with her two knives, their long straight blades dripping wet. As ferocious as we three are, there are more of them than there are of us, and I fear for our survival even as I avoid trying to see if Bridget now falls here.

"Got that bang-stick reloaded yet?" asks Dr. Sangare, stumbling back after kicking away the corpse of another jackal.

"Not quite," says Bridget. "Sorry, I just need a bit more time!"

Time is what we don't have. I turn back to see more jackals approaching, three this time. I cannot stand, my bitten leg buckles under me when I try, so from a crouch I use one leg to propel myself at one. I stumble, off balance, so the slash of my knife takes its ear off, and cuts another on the bridge of the nose. This just makes them mad, and they shake off the pain to lunge at me. Sensing the third has gotten behind me I roll out of the way. Two collide with one another, but the third jumps over them and is on me. Its heavy paws pin my arms, it slavers in my face, teeth inches from my nose.

Then it is off me, jumping high in the air like a startled cat. I sit up, knife in hand, but it is slinking away, tail between its legs. They all are—the bloodied and the whole are drawing together, bristling but submissive. I get unsteadily to my feet and hop to Bridget and Dr. Sangare, who are bitten and scratched, but alive.

"Something's spooked them," says Dr. Sangare. "They would have overwhelmed us, why..."

A sound makes us turn to the rock pile, where a shadow looms, dark against the darkening sky. Slowly it pulls itself from the rubble like some awful newborn crawling from its dead mother, and even though I can see the moon through its hazy form it seems heavy, weighted, misshapen.

"What the hell is that?" breathes Bridget, as transfixed as I.

I have no answers until the lumpy mass that appears to be its back bubbles and writhes, unfurling into two great wings. I am not the only one that recognizes it.

"Run!" shouts Dr. Sangare, as she turns and takes off. Bridget follows, slower, but slowest of all am I, limping behind with my injured leg dragging through the grass. Where they are headed I cannot say. They are not thinking those kinds of thoughts. They are only eager to be gone, and I cannot blame them.

Unlike the last time we were all running together, Dr. Sangare says nothing to encourage Bridget; does not look back at me. She is fleeing from the horrible looming thing. She does not seem to think its ephemeral nature will make it any less dangerous. Neither do I—my khukuri cannot cut smoke and shadow.

"Dily!" calls Bridget. She is struggling, the jolting of her broken forearm is taking its toll, but Dr. Sangare is not listening. She only slows momentarily when the idol falls out of her coat pocket, bouncing several times and rolling to a stop, gleaming bright in the grass. Turning on her heel, she looks at it only a moment before leaving it there.

In my mind, the color does not leave her. She is still marked for death, and as I hear a terrible flapping behind us, I sense it will come from claws as sharp as they are insubstantial.

Bridget does not have to turn back to retrieve the cursed thing. She reaches; I see the color. Her hand draws closer. I am too far behind her to stop her. Time seems to slow; before her fingertips brush the gold I see the color brightening, resolving, spreading over her. I muster my courage, and though my vision begins to swim and the colors of that twilit field grow duller I shout at her not to touch the cursed thing. I cannot sit by a second time, let it happen again.

Her fingers close on it as the beating of wings grows louder.

•

When I wake, it is night. The moon hangs huge and low above me. The first thing I feel is astonishment that I am alive. The next thing I feel is pain, all over, in my arms and legs and chest, and especially in my calf, where the jackal bit me.

I sit up, carefully, and look around. It is quiet. No shadow looms anywhere, winged and terrible.

A crumpled thing lies in the grass several yards from me. I drag myself over and see it is Bridget. She is dead, torn to pieces. The golden jackal is nowhere to be seen. I apologize to her, in my mind, for not being braver sooner. Tears roll down my cheeks as I pray she will pass quickly through the bardo and be reborn.

As I cry, I hear a sound, and I see a second figure lying in the grass. I pull myself away and limp over to find Dr. Sangare. She is no better off—worse, really, because she is still alive and clearly in great pain. She too has been torn and worried by whatever came for the idol.

She looks up at me, and smiles.

"You were right," she says. "I'm sorry."

I shake my head. I do not want an apology. It is I who should apologize—if I had mustered the courage to speak before she touched it the first time, perhaps we would not be here.

"Krishna..." she coughs. "I'm in so much pain. I know we asked you to bear so many of our burdens. Can I ask you to carry one more?"

I have never killed, never wanted to kill, but I know it would be a kindness to oblige her.

I know too that it was not the idol, nor the demon thing we saw that was destined to kill Dr. Sangare. It was me. I damned her with my inability to speak... or was it unwillingness? For the fear of a few moments' dizziness I failed to say what needed to be said, and that knowledge feels heavier than the pack I bore to Leng, the gold in the tomb... even the task that now falls to me.

I push these questions away. There is work to be done.

I smile at her, trying to apologize without words, and unsheathe my khukuri.

Molly Tanzer is the author of five novels, two novellas, and two collections of short fiction, all in the speculative mode. Her work has been nominated for the Locus Award, the British Fantasy Award, and the Wonderland Book Award; her novel *Creatures of Charm and Hunger* won the Colorado Book Award in 2021. Her shorter fictions have appeared in *The Magazine of Fantasy and Science Fiction*, *Lightspeed*, *Transcendent: The Year's Best Trans and Nonbinary Speculative Fiction*, and elsewhere. Follow her on Instagram @molly_tanzer. Molly lives outside of Boulder, CO with her notorious cat, Toad.

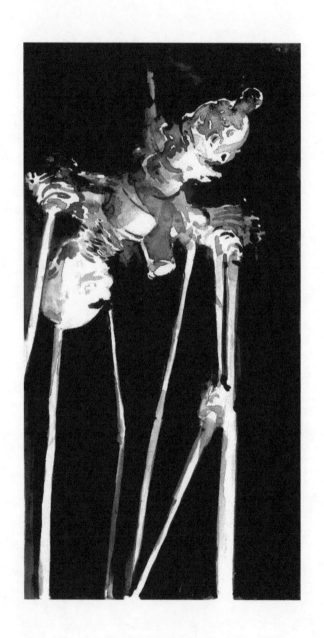

The Cancellation and Rebirth of Johannes Price

Brendan P. Bartholomew

The Berlinetta, like all modern cars, could drive itself. But Johannes Price had turned off even the most basic forms of driver-assist. This would be the last time Price drove the staggeringly expensive sports car, and he didn't want automatic braking, lane departure warnings, or electronic traction control diluting the experience. Price drove down Interstate 280 with gusto, but kept his speed below 90 mph for most of the journey. Getting pulled over by the California Highway Patrol would cost time he couldn't afford.

Though this crisis was terrifying, Price took some pleasure in how swiftly he was responding. It had been about midnight when his assistant brought the matter to his attention. Now, less than three hours later, Price was about to escape the rapidly developing nightmare.

Price had set his assistant to track any instance of his name appearing in the news or on social media. Sentient machines were still a pipe dream, but the assistant had been smart enough to code the situation as a likely public relations disaster and awaken him with an urgent alert. Groggy at first, Price had become fully awake when he realized what he was seeing. A political opinion site called Opinio displayed an image of Price's face. The origin of the photo had not been immediately apparent, but it appeared to be a still image from a low-quality video.

The accompanying headline read, "True Mathematics Exec Delivers Drunken, Racist Tirade."

Under this was a blog post from an author identified as "Nasty Michelle."

The text read, "This Silicon Valley veep is canceled! In this exclusive video from a confidential source, True Mathematics Chief Marketing Officer Johannes Price outs himself as a huge racist."

The article went on to describe the video's contents and provenance. Price's blood had turned to ice as he played the video.

"I am a Malthusian," Price said, looking directly into the camera, "Do you know what that is?"

Price had not, of course, realized he'd been looking into a camera. The constant movements made it obvious this was a piece of wearable tech, hiding in plain sight on the face of the woman he'd been addressing. What a fool he'd been.

A friend had introduced him to her at Byzantine, a San Francisco nightclub that possessed underground credibility, yet offered a VIP lounge where semi-public figures like Price could party in semi-privacy. What had her name been? Chloe or Zoey, but Price couldn't remember which. She'd been at least fifteen years his junior, and he'd felt powerfully attracted to her.

He'd liked that she wore a round piece of jewelry in the center of her forehead, in flagrant disregard of those who called it "cultural appropriation" for a white woman to wear a bindi. The decoration had gone nicely with the girl's earrings and sari-like outfit, but Price realized now the bindi had contained a camera. What a fool he'd been.

Chloe or Zoey had feigned ignorance of Price's public persona, pretending to be mostly unfamiliar with Price and his company. And she'd seemed *so* interested in his unique worldview.

Price had been drunk enough that his speech slurred in some parts of the video. Yet he had still been cagey at first, choosing his words carefully. She had placed a hand on his forearm and leaned toward him, saying, "You shouldn't be so afraid to speak your truth."

Her tightly curled brown hair had smelled wonderful. Price wasn't sure if it was perfume or just the brand of shampoo she used, but it was floral and lovely and intoxicating. She'd drawn him out, somehow subtly broaching the right topics, so he would feel safe and encouraged.

•

But how could she have known?

Price's contributions to certain political campaigns were a matter of public record, as were his guest appearances on controversial podcasts and AM talk radio programs. But Price had always been careful to portray himself as being in the mainstream, giving no hint regarding his true allegiance. Yet this girl had been on more than a random fishing expedition. It was now clear she'd known what she'd been looking for.

Had Price been careless? Had there been a leak? Had some member of the racially conscious groups he belonged to secretly been an infiltrator? Those questions would remain mysteries, as would Chloe or Zoey's true identity.

Soon it wouldn't matter.

Price exited the freeway in the hills above Menlo Park. The exit became a large, sweeping right turn, requiring motorists to complete a clockwise loop before merging onto eastbound Sand Hill Road. Price savored the g-forces pulling him sideways as he rounded the loop at an aggressive speed.

In about a minute, he was driving past the SLAC National Accelerator Laboratory, home of the Stanford Linear Accelerator. Not much of the storied campus was visible from the road, especially at night. But Price could feel the facility's presence, and it stung.

Price's title at True Mathematics did not adequately convey the pivotal role he'd played at the company. The founders were brilliant, but socially inept. It had been Price who'd helped them forge formal and informal working relationships with SLAC and other organizations, enabling a cross-pollination of ideas between those entities and the burgeoning startup. For all intents and purposes, he was a founder too.

•

Price could not pretend to truly understand atomic, solid-state, or elementary particle physics, but he'd had the audacity and people skills to get his founder-scientists in the same rooms as the researchers and venture capitalists who could help them change the world.

And now it was all coming to an end. Price would never again be welcome in SLAC's offices or laboratories. What a fool he'd been.

As Price continued east, he replayed the video in his mind. He'd already been tipsy when he'd met the girl, and he'd ordered bottle service at the dark, corner booth in which they were soon ensconced. Price had wanted to be intimate with Chloe or Zoey, and he understood now his wishful thinking, and her guile, had enabled him to believe there was intimacy and connection where there hadn't been.

When the conversation turned to the topic of race, the woman's baiting of Price had been so subtle, he still wasn't sure who'd broached the subject, not even after watching the video. What was clear was Price had well and truly screwed himself.

Sipping extravagantly priced cognac, Price had enjoyed too much the sound of his own voice as he'd shared the *for-*

bidden truths he would have never stated in the presence of a radio host, podcaster, or journalist. The girl had given him rapt attention as he'd expounded on his theories of racial science, explaining survival pressures had not vanished simply because humans had moved from hunting and gathering to living in cities.

"The welfare state has created a permanent underclass," Price said at one point in the video, "And you have to understand, for the members of this class, unwed teen pregnancy is a successful reproductive strategy."

•

If you reproduced early and often, Price had told his big-eyed new friend, it didn't matter if your poor life choices, low intelligence, or lack of resources shortened your life expectancy. All that mattered was enough of your offspring survived long enough to make babies of their own.

"Natural selection *rewards* this behavior," Price had told her.

To be honest, talking to her about "making babies" had excited him.

Had Price merely spoken in general terms about Social Darwinist concepts and the writings of Thomas Robert Malthus, it might have been possible to recover from this, to hire a crisis communications consultant to put some kind of benign spin on things while Price issued an apology, pledged to do better, and launched an initiative to help disadvantaged urban youth.

But Price had been drunk, and he'd felt safe in the presence of that adorable, approving girl, and he'd let it all out. He had specifically named the racial groups involved in the dynamic he'd been describing. In so doing, he'd left no doubt his ideas were not just a matter of economics or sociology.

Price had revealed himself, unambiguously, as a white nationalist who regarded low-income black people as a burden to society. And as the conversation had worn on, He had further disclosed his belief that financially and politically powerful Jews had weaponized black poverty, creating a kind of noblesse oblige that prevented hard-working and productive white Americans from experiencing economic and cultural freedom.

After Price had watched the video, he'd told his assistant to show him a graphical representation of the Web sites mentioning or linking to the post on Opinio. Any hope he might have had that the story could be buried or overlooked was immediately dashed.

·

He'd stood naked, watching the graphic on his bedroom's far wall, which doubled as a giant computer screen. A medium-sized red circle in the center represented Opinio. Lines radiated outward from that central icon, each one terminating in a circle representing another site that had linked to the Opinio piece.

Obscure Web sites were represented by tiny dots, while larger circles signified well-known sites with millions of readers. Many of those sites, in turn, had sprouted lines of their own, representing other pages linking to their mentions of the original Opinio essay.

The story was going viral, and Price had watched in near-real time as it spread exponentially. He'd been lucky it was all happening in the middle of the night. More than likely, the True Mathematics founders were asleep, as were the other officers of the company. This bought Price time. Maybe.

The company would have no choice but to sever its relationship with Price and then...

Then everything would come crashing down. Price had lived beyond his means. Every tangible asset he possessed had been bought on credit. And Price was about to not only lose his career, but also become unemployable and untouchable.

Price had always been good at thinking on his feet, and now his terror accelerated his thought processes. His swift actions had reflected his plan even before the plan was fully formed. The assistant had ears in every room of Price's condominium and could hear him as he tore through the home, pulling his clothes on and grabbing the items he'd need.

•

"Download to my phone and laptop every significant national news item from the United States, Europe, and all British territories from 1861 'til present day," Price had barked at the assistant, "You define 'significant,' and all files must be locally accessible with no Internet connection."

The utility pants Price had pulled on had many pockets. As he'd hurriedly stuffed those pockets, he'd added, "Same request for significant local news items from San Francisco, same date range."

Strapping on his shoulder holster and placing his SIG Sauer P320 in it, Price had placed four magazines in his pockets. Then another thought occurred to him, and he removed from its display case his reproduction Borchardt C-93 semi-automatic pistol. Price had never fired the weapon, and was therefore not in the habit of cleaning and oiling it. But he would gamble now on the proposition the gun was still in good working order. The sidearm's accompanying reproduction 7.65×25mm Borchardt cartridges were for display purposes only, but Price grabbed them too. As price placed the items in his backpack, he issued another command.

"Download to my phone and laptop all significant scientific, technical, and engineering papers from 1861 through today. You define 'significant.'"

Though devoid of consciousness, the assistant was smart enough to simulate balking at the request.

"All of them, Johannes?" it asked in the robot-sounding female voice so popular for digital assistants, "Your previous requests have used up signicant portions of both devices' internal storage."

•

"Delete most audio, video, and photo files from the historic news items," Price responded, "Keep text files only, except for stories about truly big events. You decide which ones."

Then he added, "Use all remaining storage for aforementioned science, engineering, and tech papers. Omit what you must, but try not to skimp on anything from the 19th or 20th centuries involving anesthesiology or electronics."

Price turned left on El Camino Real, continuing to agonize over the night's events, while simultaneously going through a mental checklist to be sure he hadn't forgotten anything he'd need to make his plan work. He was so lost in thought that, in about a half-mile, he realized he was not only missing his right turn on Ravenswood Avenue, but blowing through a red light. The car played a short buzzing alert sound, and the screen on the dashboard conveyed a wireless message from the intersection's red light camera, informing him he'd been dinged.

He pulled over, closed his eyes, and breathed deeply. He realized it was strategically unwise to continue driving in his current state. An accident, or encounter with the police, would create a disastrous delay. As with most things in Price's world, the premium sports car could be controlled with voice commands.

"Drive to work," Price told the vehicle.

Eleven minutes later, the Berlinetta parked itself in Price's reserved spot in front of the True Mathematics building. He grabbed his backpack off the passenger seat and strapped it on over his bomber jacket. In addition to the antique Borchardt handgun, the backpack contained Price's phone, laptop computer, compact water purifier, and first aid kit.

•

Sunrise was still at least two hours away. The company had some salaried employees who chose to come in before dawn, but probably not this early. Price approached the main entrance and waved his employee badge near the card reader. It didn't respond. Alarmed, Price rubbed his card directly on the card reader, something that shouldn't have been necessary. Now a red light lit up and the device chirped an error tone at him.

Price stood at the glass-and-chrome double doors and looked a question at the graveyard security man, who was already coming around from behind the front desk. Price's breath fogged the glass as the uniformed guard unlocked the doors and opened one just a little.

"I'm, ah... I'm very sorry Mr. Price, but we've been instructed not to let you in the building."

Price said nothing.

The guard stammered, "Mmm... uh, Mr. Morgan will be here at six o'clock. You could, uh, talk to him..."

So the CEO had locked Price out without even talking to him first. This was galling, but perhaps not a complete surprise. Morgan was probably rallying his co-founder, chief legal officer, and director of human resources at this very moment, planning to be there when Price arrived at his normal time.

The guard could have spoken to Price through the millimeter gap between the transparent double doors. Opening one door slightly had been a courtesy, designed to avoid robbing Price of all his dignity. Price appreciated the gesture, but the guard would now regret his kindness.

Price pushed the door further inward with his left hand and advanced into the lobby. The guard walked backwards, wide-eyed, putting his hands up in what might have been meant as a placating gesture. As Price advanced, he reached into his jacket, drew the Sig Sauer, and aimed it at the man.

Price wasn't sure if he'd ever seen the guard before. He was white, possibly in his late thirties, with the type of weary countenance Price associated with under-achievers who'd settled for dead-end jobs.

Like most security guards in The Valley, the man was not armed. Using armed guards was simply not the done thing. Most tech companies sought to avoid the potential massive liability problems associated with having contract employees wield deadly force, and a guard could always call the police if necessary. So the guard had no weapon to draw, and Price imagined the man was probably expecting to be taken hostage.

"I'm sorry about this," Price said, and fired his gun.

At the shooting range, the Sig Sauer had always sounded like a firecracker. But the accoustics of the lobby amplified the sound into a thunderclap that reverberated through the building before the guard hit the floor.

Price removed the guard's employee badge from its lanyard belt clip, then rifled through the man's pockets and retrieved his building keys.

Price knew there were other guards on duty, and they would have heard the gunshot. The front doors having been unlocked and opened would show on the guards' digital assistants even if Price locked them now, so the guards would likely converge on the lobby.

Price's pulse pounded almost audibly in his head as he jogged up the stairs to the mezzanine level. His breathing become rapid and labored as he badged a door open and entered a corridor.

Price had truly passed the point of no return. Prior to firing that gun, he had still possessed the option of continuing to live his life. He would have been destitute and socially outcast, and might also have been prosecuted when his use of company funds to cover personal debts was discovered. But Price would have still had some kind of life. A terrible, downgraded life, but a life.

As Price traversed the hallways, badging himself through additional doors, going inwards toward the heart of the facility, his field of vision seemed to tilt, as if the world itself were off-kilter.

One decision can change your whole life, Price thought.

Finally Price arrived at the room the company had humorously dubbed The Sanctum Santorum. The guard's badge unlocked the glass outer door, which slid aside into the wall, just like the doors on space ships in science fiction movies. Most employee badges could not unlock the doors to the Sanctum, but for safety reasons, the security staff had access.

What was inside had not yet been revealed to the world, but in the unlikely event a guard had entered, he or she could not possibly have recognized the room's most exotic contents for what they were.

•

Price entered the airlock and the door re-closed behind him. There were cameras in every ceiling, and the surviving security staff was surely watching him at this point. The airlock was designed to keep dust and germs out. It would offer no resistance to the police who were surely en route, if not already entering the building.

Price opened the inner door and stepped through.

There it was.

The time machine.

The clean room's floor space was roughly equivalent to that of a high school gymnasium, with a ceiling high enough that the room occupied three stories of the building. In the center was a small, circular, raised stage, coated in a highly reflective material. Perched above the stage was a large, black machine on stilts. Spiderlike, it resembled the complicated, multi-lens projectors that had been used in planetariums before advances in curved wall screen technology rendered them obsolete.

The machine was much larger than a planetarium projector, however, and its height was what had necessitated the use of a space with such a tall ceiling. Thick, heavily insulated power cables extended from one corner of the room, running up one leg of the giant spider and connecting to its body.

Other than this, the rest of the room was quite unremarkable. The stage and unusual machine were surrounded by two rings of computer workstations, all facing inward. Price had always wanted the space to look something like a

NASA mission control room, with purpose-built computer terminals, giant wall screens, myriad flashing lights, and lots of technicians concentrating intensely while speaking into their headsets. Instead, the workstations and chairs were off-the-shelf items from Office Depot, bearing perfectly mundane-looking desktop computers.

The scene had always reminded Price of the kind of avant-garde theater space where the seats are arranged in circles around the stage, allowing the performers to be viewed from every angle. Anything placed on this stage would give only one type of performance; a disappearing act. Unless, of course, if it has been "previously" placed on the stage and sent back from the future. In which case it would appear, rather than disappear.

Price had never possessed an aptitude for math, physics, philosophy, or any other thing that might have prevented his head from hurting when he thought about the logistics of time travel. No, getting smart people together and enabling them to work their magic was Price's talent. He'd always loved to make deals, promote things, and be entrepreneurial. Price didn't need to understand how time travel worked. He had only needed to convince the right investors that his people might really be able to do it.

Price's hand shook as he threw the large switch that would send power to the machine. The device's low, resonant hum quietly filled the room. It was a sound easily drowned out by loud conversation, and its subtlety seemed to convey the black metal arachnid's awesome, world-changing power. It was as if the machine was saying, *I don't have to make a lot of noise. You know what I can do.*

Price removed his backpack, set it on the floor, and sat at one of the computers. Other than typing in his username and password, most of what he needed to do could be accomplished by pointing and clicking. Price was the farthest thing from an expert, but the operations team had previously granted him the ceremonial honor of operating the machine during one of its inaugural tests.

·

As Price clicked various items on the interface, his phone suddenly began to ring from within his backpack. The sound was jarring, shrill, and alarming. This would be the police, who'd surely surrounded the building. The security staff had no doubt retrieved Price's phone number from the employee directory. Or, perhaps, Morgan had provided it.

The police would be calling in the hope they could talk him into surrendering himself. Price thought of answering the phone in order to buy himself some time.

No.

No, no, no.

He needed to focus. He reached into the backpack and turned the phone off.

He should have powered the phone down much sooner, in order to conserve its battery. But the thing was less than a year old, and a top-of-the-line model, boasting a battery life measured in years. By the time his phone was ready to die, Price might very well have gotten some smart people together in a room and convinced them to build him something capable of recharging the device.

The interface Price worked with was a marvel of elegant simplicity. He knew there were a maddening number of complicated settings and equations that needed to be adjusted each time the machine was used, but the interface distilled them all into just two top-level questions: *When and where?*

Price understood space and time were somehow inextricably linked, that one did not travel in space or in time, but in *spacetime*. Nevertheless, the interface asked the user for two separate settings. "When" was one set of coordinates, and "where" was the other.

·

The "when" part was much easier for Price to grasp, because it was perfectly linear. Physicists might claim time was a circle, hologram, curved line, or any number of other weird things, but the interface only required the user to imagine time as a straight line and choose where on the line he wanted to send something.

Beneath the graphical user interface, the system could allow the user to type commands that would select a teraannum, gigaannum, megaannum, millennium, century, year, month, day, hour, minute, second, millisecond, microsecond, nanosecond, picosecond, and femtosecond. Thankfully, the window Price was working with kept things much simpler, only asking for a year, month, date, hour, minute, and second.

The "where" part was far more complicated, because it could not be imagined as a straight line. Geography and geometry were additional fields Price had never truly grasped, and as simplified as the location window might have been, it still asked for a baffling array of coordinates in more than three dimensions. He would have to roll the dice and not adjust the location.

The True Mathematics campus wasn't built on landfill like the offices and laboratories east of the Bayshore Freeway, so Price wasn't in danger of appearing in the Bay, dozens of meters from the shoreline. If Price materialized in a redwood tree the result would be catastrophic. But he simply had no time to figure out the location settings in order to minimize that risk.

So the "where" of things was Menlo Park. Regardless of which calendar date he chose, Price would go on a long journey to this exact spot, 30 miles south of San Francisco.

•

Traveling to the future was out of the question. Having no information on future events, Price couldn't be sure this space wouldn't be replaced by some new building with different dimensions. And materializing in space occupied by a wall would be just as deadly as trying to occupy a tree's space.

Furthermore, traveling to the future would only confer disadvantages. The time projector would retain a record of its most recent settings, so Price would materialize surrounded by people aware of his crimes and expecting his arrival.

Even without that problem, what advantage could a man from the past possibly have? Regardless of where in the future Price appeared, he would show up ignorant of history and possessing no knowledge or technology not already possessed by that era's natural inhabitants.

So the past it would be.

The question of when was an interesting one.

Earlier, Price had briefly, but not seriously, entertained a fantasy in which he did the local Native Americans a favor, arrived prior to the European conquest, and warned them of the coming invasion. This could have involved arriving just prior to Columbus' 1492 sea voyage, but Columbus and his contemporaries had spent so much time mired in the islands or the Central American mainland that Price arriving in 1491 would have felt like Price arriving unnecessarily early.

In a more reasonable and relevant version of the fantasy, Price had imagined himself appearing in 1765, making contact with the Ohlone, teaching them how to speak English, and upgrading their weapons technology.

•

On November 1, 1769, when José Francisco Ortega climbed to the top of Sweeney Ridge and discovered the San Francisco Bay, Price and his band of Indians, now a capable military force, would be waiting for him. They would decapitate Ortega and instruct the surviving members of his party to carry a message back to Gaspar de Portolà.

"Tell the Governor that Alta California belongs to me," Price imagined himself saying, "Tell him our hills and deserts have rich gold and silver deposits, but Spaniards will never see them without paying tribute to my army."

As a boy, Price had been bullied, abused, and neglected by the students and staff of a middle school bearing Ortega's name. Killing Ortega would have felt like some great cosmic reckoning, like a long over-due act of revenge that, amazingly, would prevent the original grievance from ever happening.

Those harms in Price's personal history would never come to pass, and yet they had, and would always be. This was because the Grandfather Paradox did not exist.

Prior to True Mathematics' founding, some deep thinkers had asserted that if you were a time traveler, you did not have to worry you might go back in time, accidentally kill your grandfather, and thus prevent yourself from ever existing. They claimed if you killed your grandfather prior to your own birth, the moment at which you had arrived in the past became the moment you sprang into existence, fully formed, with intact memories of an alternate timeline which would now never be, but upon which *your* existence no longer depended.

The company had conducted experiments validating this theory. Without killing anybody, of course.

•

It would be a while before Price could even begin to process his feelings about the homicide he'd just committed, but he believed the moment he stepped into the past, he would set in motion a timeline where that security guard would never be killed, but would also be born into different circumstances than the ones he'd experienced in this world, if he were still to be born at all.

Price could not believe the mere act of traveling in time could split the universe in two, creating alternate timelines that would exist alongside each other. The idea of a multiverse was just too ridiculous and fanciful. Regardless, the timeline Price was fleeing would be completely inaccessible from the one he would enter. Even if the original timeline still existed in some place other than Price's memory, it might as well not.

New sounds appeared over the low hum of the time machine. Price heard the dull thuds of booted footfalls, and the muted sounds of men yelling indistinctly. Though an airlock protected the large, windowless room, its walls contained no special insulation against sound. Police officers were in the building.

Price got up and stood directly beneath an inverted dome in the ceiling, which contained the room's security cameras. He fired a tight cluster of three rounds into the device, which rained metal, plastic, and glass debris. He hated to lose bullets and risk damaging the time machine with a ricochet. But he'd needed to deprive the police of the ability to see into the room, and the loud gunshots would give them pause.

Price retrieved his backpack from the floor, leaned over the workstation, and clicked the icon that would activate the system's natural speech assistant.

•

"Can you hear me?" Price asked.

"Yes," the system replied, in another variation on the ubiquitous robot-sounding female voice.

"I'm going to enter a date, but I will not be in front of the computer when it's time to send," Price told the artificial intelligence, "Therefore, I want you to send when I speak the words 'sun wheel.' Do you understand?"

"Yes," the machine replied, "Send will commence when user says 'sun wheel.'"

Now his decision would become real.

As much as Price had enjoyed his fantasy about leading the Indians, who would revere him as a godlike savior, he would have felt too isolated, being the only white man among thousands of natives. Price enjoyed thinking of them as "Indians," and not "Native Americans," for the same reason he'd liked Chloe or Zoey's wearing a bindi and Hindu-themed outfit despite her being white. If the social justice warriors said you weren't allowed to do something, Price felt you were serving the greater good by doing whatever that thing was.

His covert investment in the principles of white separatism notwithstanding, Price bore the Indians no ill will. But Price's beliefs rested on foundations laid by the French aristocrat, Count Joseph Arthur De Gobineau, and the Nazi theorist, Alfred Rosenberg. He therefore regarded Indians as belonging to a lower order of Man. And hadn't Price expended enough time and energy adjusting to other cultures?

•

Indeed, from the very moment the plan had begun to form, one date had burned in Price's mind. He leaned over the computer terminal again, hands now trembling as much with excitement as with terror and trauma. Price entered the date April 12th, 1861.

Then Price strode with confidence toward the raised, circular stage in the center of the room. This was the first time he'd felt truly self-assured since the whole crazy emergency had begun.

Price again heard the sound of men yelling indistinctly, and saw movement on the far side of the airlock's glass doors. The airlock was narrow enough the police would be forced to enter almost in single-file, Price thought, and he assumed they'd be cautious about doing so, lest they make easy targets of themselves.

But whatever the cops were planning, it would happen soon.

Price's destination made perfect sense. 1861 was early enough that the scientific and technical information he bore would come as powerful revelations. But 1861 was also so recent, some of the era's inhabitants would be learned enough to understand what Price offered, and have the skills and resources to do something about it. And in 1861, Price would find himself among English-speaking Americans, in a culture he understood.

More to the point, April 12, 1861 was the day Southern forces began the Civil War by firing upon Fort Sumter. Price had not cared much about history prior to his involvement in racial consciousness, but the Civil War had become an obsession for him.

Price imagined news from the East Coast regarding the war's first shots might be slow to reach Northern California. He knew Western Union's trans-continental telegraph service wouldn't link San Francisco to Washington, D.C. prior to October 1861, so word of the momentous conflict in Charleston could take a while to reach the busy port city.

•

How long it would take Price to reach San Francisco was another question. A map and route query had indicated a person in the present day could hike from Menlo Park to San Francisco in 10.5 hours of uninterrupted walking, but Price doubted the proposed route would exist in 1861.

El Camino Real would exist in some unpaved form, but Price was unsure as to whether the road's location back then would be the same as in the present. Regardless, Price knew he couldn't hike 30 miles in one day. Just making the journey on horseback in those days had surely been a grueling, all-day affair.

Price assumed he would appear in a woodland area, or perhaps a marsh, and have to hike east or west before he found El Camino or some other road. Then he would try to find somebody with a horse or horse-drawn wagon to give him a ride.

Price figured the multi-tool he carried, or his wristwatch, would be sufficient barter to secure transportation. He hoped so, anyway, because he was traveling light, and couldn't spare many of the other things he carried. Price would, of course, require food and lodging, but he could not conceive of himself hiring on somewhere as a laborer.

If his plan hadn't developed on the spur of the moment, if Price had had the luxury of a few days' head start, he could have visited an antique coin dealer and stocked up on vintage currency from the era.

But hadn't this plan already existed in some abstract form, if Price was being completely honest with himself? Hadn't his daydreams and fantasies mapped the path he now followed, long before this night's crisis had forced him into motion?

•

Price would go to San Francisco, identify people of means sympathetic to the Confederacy, and convince them to send him to the South with funds and letters of introduction. Persuading them would not be difficult. Showing a person one video clip on his phone or laptop would prove Price had come from the future.

Price wanted to be careful about revealing himself, however, and had in mind some subtler strategies. Spiritualism, séances, automatic writing, and ouija boards would not capture the public consciousness until after the Civil War, but Price assumed the San Francisco of 1861 contained at least a few well-heeled socialites who believed in psychic powers and talking to the dead.

He would find such people and privately disclose to them prophecies of the very near future. As soon as stories consistent with his predictions appeared in the papers, his marks would be convinced of his supernatural powers. And then Price would have his patrons. He imagined he could extract enough wealth from such benefactors to finance a southward journey even without identifying Confederate-sympathizers.

Price knew it would be impossible to reach Montgomery before the Confederate States of America moved its capital to Richmond, but he thought he might make for Montgomery anyway. Traveling to either city by land would be hellish, but Montgomery was closer. Price wasn't sure which city would be easier to reach by sea, but he knew a ship journey would be another kind of ordeal.

Had Price been interested only in enriching himself, remaining in the North and aiding the Union would have been far less trouble, and just as lucrative. But Price cared about the greater good, and the prospect of changing the outcome of the Civil War was an opportunity from which he could not shrink.

•

He had so much to offer. The Sig Sauer would demonstrate the stunning advantage of a self-loading pistol that didn't need to be cocked before each pull of the trigger, but its internal mechanisms and machining would be hard to emulate using mid-19th century processes. The Borchardt C-93 in Price's backpack, however, was a precise reproduction of a gun designed in 1893. It had been the world's first semi-automatic pistol, and when Price presented it to President Jefferson Davis, General Robert E. Lee, or some other Confederate official, they would immediately see the possibility of it.

The Borchardt would be easy to understand, reverse-engineer, and manufacture.

And then there were the Confederate battle losses. Price would describe the staggering death tolls at places like Antietam, explain what had gone wrong, and thus enable the South to avoid those failures. The gratitude Price would receive from the Confederate generals and elected officials would be indescribable.

And what a glorious experiment this would be. Would slavery naturally fall by the wayside, even after a Confederate victory? Some writers denigrated as "revisionists" believed the institution would have soon been phased out even with no war.

The thought that hundreds of thousands of American boys and men had been slaughtered or maimed to achieve an outcome that would have arrived anyway was deeply offensive to Price's sense of morality. How many lives would be saved by a quick, decisive Southern victory? Time would tell.

•

Price stepped up onto the highly reflective stage. It occurred to him to strap his backpack on, but he didn't want to take the time. Holding the backpack's straps in his right hand, Price addressed the room in a grand, commanding voice.

"Sun wheel."

Nothing happened.

Price was about to demand an explanation when the system's robot-girl voice said, "CAUTION: Location values have not been entered."

"Yes, I know," Price bit back, trying to control his voice, "We are going to send without adjusting the location; do you understand?"

"Yes," the system replied.

The airlock's doors slid open and a deep, electronically amplified male voice filled the Sanctum. "Mr. Price, I need you to throw your gun across the room and get down on the floor, face down, hands away from your body."

Price could see a S.W.A.T. operator in thick, black body armor on the other side of the airlock, flattened against a wall, using the narrow frame of the outer door as a partial blind. Price couldn't see the other operators, but could feel them, poised to invade the room. A flash-bang grenade or tear gas would surely precede their incursion, leaving him disoriented and the time machine potentially damaged and inoperable.

Some crazed, fearful part of him commandeered his inner voice, urging him to give up while he still could.

Price ignored the panic trying to bloom within him. He stood erect, looked right at the S.W.A.T. operator, and proudly spoke the words, "SUN WHEEL."

•

Everything went black and silent, just as Price had expected.

Motion pictures and virtual reality experiences always subjected viewers to dazzling light shows when depicting time travel, but reality was quite the opposite. True Mathematics had not yet sent a person through time, but they'd sent a camera, and its audio and video recordings had borne out what the theorists had predicted: Light and sound waves depended on time, and could not be perceived by a viewer traveling outside the figurative medium of spacetime.

So Price was not at all surprised by the abrupt moment of no light and no sound. But then, suddenly, there were light sources, and everything was shockingly violent and strange.

Urine and gas evacuated Price's body, but he barely noticed, because his lungs felt like they were on fire and trying to push his esophagus and tongue through his teeth. For a fraction of an instant, Price tried to believe this might be a normal, if unexpected part of the time-send experience.

But then Price's backpack floated up before his eyes.

The backpack was a black silhouette against the backdrop of light sources, which also moved upward, relative to Price's point of view.

Dear God, they looked like...

They couldn't be.

It couldn't be.

Then a massive, reddish-orange, curved line scrolled up into Price's field of view. Everything below the line was black, and blocking the backdrop of pinprick light sources. Price realized then he was looking at the corona of the Earth, which was between him and the sun.

Even as this realization came, Price's vision fogged, depriving him of the most majestic view he'd ever experienced. Were his eyes desiccating as their surface water boiled off? Or had the water rapidly frozen? Price was only peripherally aware of the question.

The cold, unthinking computer-girl voice rang out in Price's mind:

"CAUTION: Location values have not been entered."

Of course. Of course, of course, of course.

There were precessional changes in Earth's orbit. So much so, it was probably sheer happenstance Price had even appeared close enough to have a view of the planet.

Price continued to tumble, but his vision was so clouded, he couldn't even see the stars transiting his field of view.

What a fool he'd been.

Brendan Bartholomew was diagnosed with a processing difficulty at the age of sixteen, but never received any help for it. His writing has appeared in The San Francisco Examiner, SF Weekly, CityLab, The San Mateo Daily Journal, "Best of Temp Slave!" and "The Factsheet Five Zine Reader." Brendan is a lifelong Bay Area resident, and works as a bus driver for the city of San Francisco.

What Was I Scared of?

Scott Nicolay

As a child, I had a fascination with all things monstrous, ghostly, and macabre, with every kind of creepy crawling thing. As far as I know, I was born that way—I have no memory of any formative moment that imprinted me with this proclivity. Instead, my earliest memories relate to my fixation on dinosaurs, ghosts, and monsters. One of these memories comes from a party at my grandparents' house, where someone gifted me a cocktail napkin imprinted—in extravagant polychrome typography—with the words of the "Quaint Old Litany" that Alfred Noyes first published in 1908: "From Ghoulies and Ghoosties, long-leggety Beasties, and Things that go Bump in the Night, Good Lord, deliver us!"[1]

---

1   Although Noyes (1880-1958) offered no specific attribution for this

The ecstasy I experienced upon first hearing this snippet of verse has not altogether faded over the intervening decades. I spent the rest of that evening begging every adult within reach to reread the text to me and losing myself in visions of just what these Things and Beasties might look like. I sought no deliverance from the Lord: images of long-leggety Beasties transported me instead.

Little did I know then that at least one of these napkin apparitions already had, or at least would one day manifest its own real-world counterpart, its very objective correlative. Even less could I have anticipated the singularly eerie night my friend Greg Roemer-Baer and I would spend over half a century later and on the opposite side of the continent, camped out high in the western Sierra Nevadas in hopes of an encounter with just such a long-leggety Beastie as Noyes had invoked over a century earlier.

It was another friend, Melissa Eisner, who first told me about the Fresno Nightcrawler not long after I moved to California in 2016. Melissa owns and manages Coffee Bandits, my favorite local coffeehouse, and I have a reasonably clear memory of our original discussion on the topic occurring at her establishment. Although I cannot recall the conversational context in which it arose, I do recall my initial befuddlement, followed shortly afterward by astonishment

---

text, he may have drawn it from Welsh tradition, as he lived in the venerable Cardiganshire town of Aberystwyth from the age of 4 until his departure for Oxford 14 years later. His contemporary Oliver Onions (1873-1961) used a variation of the same text just three years later as the epigraph to his iconic collection *Widdershins*.

and delight when I looked up the video footage to which she had referred me online and watched it.

For reasons that will shortly become obvious, from this point forward I shall refer to the entity in question as the Fresno Night*walker*, not the Fresno Night*crawler*. Nightwalker*s*, for that matter, since both videoclips show more than one—unlike Nessie, Champie, and the Jersey Devil, the Fresno Nightwalker has never been a monad. Thus I shall primarily refer to *them* in the plural hereinafter, unless specific context dictates otherwise, for instance when I make reference to the social phenomenon and/or the concept rather than the bipedal figures that appear in the recordings.

The entirety of the evidence for the Fresno Nightcrawler's existence consists of two short grainy videoclips, both recorded at night on security or wildlife cameras. The two clips show similar brief scenes of a pair of pale figures walking (not crawling) down a gently sloping hillside. The first was recorded on private property in Fresno, and the second in Yosemite National Park. To the best of my knowledge, no reliable information exists to confirm the provenience of either recording. The figures appear to be little more than pairs of legs surmounted by what might be small round heads, though they exhibit no eyes or other facial features. No arms or torsos either. They walk slowly, stiffly, very much like crude puppets (are you out there, Thomas Ligotti?). Both recordings look equally and obviously fake, even ridiculously so.

Over the past few years, the "Fresno Nightcrawler" has become the focus of cottage industry of sorts. One can purchase a variety of paraphernalia and depictions related to this figure that now inhabits the public domain. Meanwhile, although both recordings are still available to view on online, they have become somewhat more difficult to locate. Internet searches now bring up mainly secondary footage, which is to say whereas one could until recently easily watch both of the original one-minute clips, these are now mostly only available embedded in longer explanatory videos, requiring the viewer to wade through ten or more minutes of commentaries by various earnest-seeming young white men in order to see the good stuff. None of these commentaries have anything of value to offer, as no legitimate additional evidence or information about the Nightwalkers exists outside the two original clips. The inaccessibility of primary archival material compromises any attempts at determining the provenience and relative validity of these recordings.

An additional point deserves note: the Nightwalkers in both videoclips appear to be shrouded in pale fabric, making them resemble Halloween ghost decorations. Many viewers describe them as resembling pants walking by themselves. Of course, this contributes to the initial impression that the recordings are hoaxes. However, the longer one observes the Nightwalkers, the more their odd bifurcated shape and their peculiar style of ambulation combine to create a distinctly uncanny impression. In fact, this may be one of the most singularly apt applications of the word "uncanny" that I have encountered. The more times one watches either or both of the clips, the more unsettling they become. Herein lies the fascination of the Fresno Nightwalkers. Fake they probably—almost certainly—are, but how would someone go about faking something like this, and *why*?

The Fresno Nightwalkers evoked for me another very early memory from my childhood, one perhaps even earlier than that of the Noyes napkin: the image of pants walking through the woods by themselves, altogether uninhabited. This image will likely register with familiarity to some readers, as it did the first time I saw the footage of our friends from Fresno. Watching the Nightwalkers recalled a memory of my mother reading to me while we sat together on the wooden stairway to the upper floor of my hometown library. This was the original town library, a musty and haunted-looking old house that stood alone facing the main street of our town, between the high school and the woods along the brook, which is to say the brook that runs through the middle of town, as opposed to the other brooks that define its borders. Behind that structure a lush green park stretched back to more woods and the old sewage treatment plant. I set my story "The Bad Outer Space" in that park. The high school, the sewage treatment plant, and the woods on two sides of the park also figure in that story, and they all remain in the same locations today. The town must have torn down the library in the early seventies, although I have no specific memory of its destruction. All I can recall is that at some point in my early youth, a new library opened between the rescue squad building and the borough hall, and the old library disappeared.

I vaguely remember that my mother was reading to me that day because she wanted to take my mind off something.

Perhaps I had just been to the doctor for a shot. Maybe I had just found out I was soon to have a brother (if the latter, I could not have been much more than two years old, which seems about right). I also have the barest memory of requesting a scary book or maybe a book about ghosts. Maybe not so much a memory as simply the secure knowledge of my predilections at that age. The book the librarian brought us, and which my mother read aloud to me there on the stairs, was—and this is the part I remember most clearly, certainly the reason I remember that day at all—*What Was I Scared Of?* by Dr. Seuss.

Other writers in the weird fiction literary community also recall the power of their encounters with this book, which I know because it became a frequent topic of discussion on my interview podcast, *The Outer Dark*. For those unfamiliar with this iconic and canonical work, *What Was I Scared Of?* relates the experience of a person—not a human being exactly, but one of Seuss' ubiquitous anthropomorphic mammalian amalgams—who encounters an ambulatory pair of "pale green pants" with no one inside them walking along a dark forest path one night. Curiously, the genderless protagonist wears no pants or clothes of any kind, which adds a further undercurrent of cognitive dissonance to the narrative. The pants pursue the narrator through a variety of landscapes, all rendered almost entirely in eerie hues of blue and green. The original Fresno recording of the Nightwalkers has a bluish cast overall. The Yosemite clip is green.

How strange then that fate would bring me all these many years later to a land where creatures bearing an uncanny resemblance to ol' Doc Seuss's pants with no one in them stroll down the hillsides at night. Almost immediately after Melissa told me about the Fresno Nightcrawler, I conceived a simple and elegant plan via which one might optimize the chances of encountering these beings in person. My plan hinged on the simple fact that only two sightings of these entities exist. This rather unique circumstance in the world of cryptozoology pointed to an equally unique way to search for the Nightwalkers, an approach that would be, if not quite scientific, at least systematic. And at least worth a shot. Because even though everyone has seen the video footage, no one has seen a Fresno Nightwalker. Not with their own eyes. How did we think we might become the first(s)?

Well, cryptozoologist Loren Coleman, he has an interesting theory that he uses to explain the statistical anomalies associated with cryptid encounters, UFO sightings, and various other Fortean anomalies. A pair of theories, really, though I should note that these are "theories" in the popular sense of untested explanations rather than in the scientific sense of tested hypotheses.

Early in his career, Coleman began compiling data on cryptid sightings and other Fortean events, which led him to make two interesting claims, which he first described in detail in his books *Curious Encounters* and *Mysterious America*. The first is that locations with sinister names like Devil's Backbone or Satan's Armpit have a higher incidence of Fortean events such as cryptid and UFO sightings. This pattern also includes some less obvious place names, such as Logan, Reeves, Lafayette, and Fayetteville (regarding the last two Coleman further suggested that any site containing the syllable "fay" might be a locus of Fortean activity).

Coleman also noted that these events tend to cluster in time as well as space, and that specific dates seem to function as strange attractors in much the same way as specific locations. The centerpiece of this second theory or claim is that the peak date of occurrence for all such events falls on June 24, the Nativity of John the Baptist. Coleman even connects these two theories at times, for instance by noting that at least a dozen prominent people associated with UFOs and Ufology have died on June 24, including *Loren Janes* (1931-2017), Kirk Douglas' stunt double in *Spartacus* who later coordinated stunts for the film *Repo Man*. Loren Janes also played a character named "Coleman" in the 1966 film *The Sand Pebbles*.[2] Apparently when the going gets weird, it can get personal, too.

With Coleman's theories in mind, Greg and I set out for the Sierra Nevadas on the evening of June 24, 2021. Obviously our choice of date was neither random nor accidental. Nor was our destination. My thinking was that given the existence of only two sightings of the Nightwalkers, one from Fresno and one from Yosemite, then the ideal way to spot one of these entities, according to Coleman's theories, would be to locate the spot between these two locations with the most infernal name and spend the night of John the Baptist's birthday there. Greg and I planned to

---

2   Following this rabbit hole a bit further, I discovered that Richard McKenna, the author of the original novel *The Sand Pebbles*, also wrote science fiction. His story "The Secret Place," published posthumously in Damon Knight's first anthology in the *Orbit* series, won the Nebula Award for Best Short Story in 1966. It's a fine example of Weird Fiction that is not horror, although it certainly does evoke dread.

ascend into the Sierras on this specific night to maximize our chances of seeing the Fresno Nightcrawler. Although I had formulated this plan of action several years earlier, my first three years in California always found me conducting archaeological fieldwork out of state, or even out of the country on that date. I need not elaborate on why we hadn't made the trip during the previous summer. Therefore, this was the first, and perhaps the only year I could put my plan into action. Things, as they are wont to do however, took on a complication even before we left. The night before our planned excursion, Greg messaged me to say that he had "almost" bailed out on the trip. Almost. But not quite.

It was not until we pulled out of his driveway near Visalia and began the journey to our campsite that Greg told me the story why he had almost cancelled. By the time he had completed his narration, I too was having second thoughts about the whole operation.

Most of Greg's story takes place at a remote research station located in Sequoia National Park. The Park Service has assigned the area a "Wilderness" designation. This affords it the highest level of protection. No wheeled vehicles, no complex machines are allowed. The cabin is the staging area for the ongoing exploration of R—— Cave, a gated cave on Park Service land. Greg has been part of the R—— Cave project for seven years. It's his passion.

July 4 was going to be the big expedition back to the cave, the first since the pandemic. Greg had visited the cabin in advance and had noticed that it was down on stocks: low on water, low on firewood, and half the shingles had been half ripped off by a bear. Bears stay away from the cabin when people are there, but with no one around for almost two years, at least one bear must have gotten curious. So Greg combined the idea of stocking the cabin with the idea of taking his stepson William on a backwoods excursion, something they both had been talking about. The plan was to spend three days and two nights, get everything done, all the wood-chopping, all the repairs, all the stocking.

Apparently Greg's wife, Cassie, also didn't want him to go ahead with our Nightwalker search trip after he and William had returned and he told her how things had gone at the cabin. But in the end, he decided to go. He told me later he decided to go for the same reason he goes caving. Because if there is something to see he wants to see it.

I will let Greg tell his own story[3] from here:

3   I present Greg's story here in his own words. Although I did not take notes when he first told it that evening in the truck, I interviewed him several months later and transcribed what follows above from that interview. He retold the story then in almost exactly the same words and in all the same particulars as I remembered, and my memory of the original telling is vivid enough that I probably could have written it here without the interview. The only edits are for smoothness, clarity, and syntax: except for deliberately obscuring place names and other sensitive information in order to protect sensitive sites and environments—as well as those who might endanger themselves and others in the attempts to visit those sites—I made no alterations to the actual content of the story. There is a single addition to this version that Greg did relate on June 24, 2021, which is the part near the end wherein William and Kayla "compared notes" regarding their separate experiences at the cabin. Greg remained unaware of that detail until after our trip. Greg did relate some events during the October interview that occurred after our June 24 trip into the Sierras. These included ominous experiences that Cas-

I had this idea of taking William out and giving him a little bit of a taste of the outdoors while getting some work done that needed to be done. I talked to him about it first and told him that would be an option. I didn't want to drag him along and surprise him with it, but he was actually pretty excited to do it. So we were just going to get everything done, all the wood chopping, all the repairs, and get the cabin in shape for July 4.

Because of the Wilderness designation, everything's on foot, so we had to park at the trailhead and hike five miles down to the research station with all our supplies and packs, just as we do for caving expeditions. And you know, when he arrived at the cabin for his first time seeing it, he was pretty excited.

We decided to have a bit of a snack and get right to work. Since we'd left pretty early, we were able to spend all day dragging firewood out of the forest. We were allowed to take dead and down, but we had to process it using hand tools. We had a two-person saw. The misery whip.

Things went well, and after a while we're pretty well stocked on firewood, and we'd gotten most of the repairs done. It got to be about twilight, and we're winding down for the day, I'm thrilled by how well everything has gone. We have dinner. Everything is pretty normal. William's

---

sie had when she returned to the research station, and Greg's close encounter with some large creature, probably a bear, scratching at the outhouse door while he was inside. I have omitted those events from the primary narrative, and touch on them here only to clarify the editorial decisions I made in transcribing the interview.

been asking me what does it take to go in the cave, what kind of training does he need to do, and we're having that discussion.

But I still had to haul in some water. I had done a trip last winter running some paleoclimatology equipment, and we had used most of the little bit of the water that was left. For water we had to go another mile and a half all the way down the trail to the spring and get seven gallons from there, and then I ended up going in-cave and retrieving another seven gallons out of the cave stream.

So the last two years on the project I have slept outside in a hammock. Anywhere else, I always sleep in the hammock, but in the cabin it's been kind of traditional that everybody sleeps inside in the loft. I really don't sleep well around a bunch of people though. The loft is basically like an attic; it's just a big flat space above the main body of the cabin, just flat wood and 10 people lying there on pads and sleeping bags, all in the same space. That's kind of to establish what I usually do out there, and in what stark contrast that stands to how things are about to go in the next five minutes so.

I guess rather than adding it later, maybe now's a good time.

I've lived here all my life. I've been hiking in in the back country in the Sierra since I was 15. I've put in easily by now, I don't know probably 1500 miles on foot in those mountains. I've done all manner of hiking solo, all manner of hiking solo at night, sometimes hiking solo at night navigating by moonlight and sometimes only starlight. I've had any number of bear and wildlife encounters. Effectively, what

I'm trying to establish here is that those mountains are for all intents and purposes, home to me.

There are things out there I have a healthy respect for. Nothing that scares me in the sense I'm about to describe.

Caving is my life. That cabin and that cave are the center of it. At no point have I ever had any kind of oddness in that cave, in the midst of all this, or at any point earlier. Any strangeness of that area was absolutely not tied to the cave itself.

That place above else is literally like a second home to me. I have felt nothing but at home and at peace there.

And I don't spook easily.

I certainly have seen some weirdness on expeditions elsewhere, in Mexico, deep in the jungle, things that were very strange, very unsettling. But even those things didn't rise to the level of where this is about to head.

It's nighttime, probably about 10:00 o'clock.

I zipped myself in my hammock.[4]

I looked over to the left at a full, very yellow moon coming through the trees and...I was suddenly overcome by a really, suddenly...I'm trying to think of a good word for a severe really pronounced, compulsion, just like *GET THE FUCK OUT NOW*.

It's hard to describe in any other terms than that.

---

4   Greg uses the same ultralight backpacking hammock that I swear by for jungle archaeology especially, the Hennessey Expedition Asymmetric. These hammocks have built in mosquito-netting on the top, are super-tough, only weigh about one kg., and roll up in your pack to about the size of a medium haggis.

Beyond not being very prone to fear and getting spooked, I'm also not prone to having impulses in my head that are, you know, presenting so strongly that there's almost no override. Whatever this was, it was an imperative: it was like get the fuck out of here straightaway right now get in the cabin. Which I did. Took me all of three seconds.

There wasn't anything else. Nothing I actually saw or heard. Nothing other than that feeling. But it was horrifically strong.

Now I'm inside and trying my level best to keep a poker face. I just told William I had decided to sleep on the floor.

The first thing William said was I am so glad you came in. I didn't know how you'd respond. There is something really weird and off. I was just about to come get you and ask you to come inside and stay inside.

Right then I got a little more serious about staying inside. Shuttered the place up. Closed all the shutters. Secured the door with rope, tied off to large nails in the doorframe. Normally it's wide open for ventilation, but we weren't having any fires. We have some heavy objects in the cabin, we call them the A Box and the B Box, and a series of other boxes, called the coffins. They're old, maybe 1960s Navy issue latching transport cases for modular radar equipment that H—— brought in. We use those for storage in the cabin. I moved those in front of the door.

I had initially tried to do the whole "everything is fine, I'm just coming in" routine. We had just had a really normal positive uneventful day, absolutely nothing going on, nothing out of the ordinary happening, everything good, everything positive.

To have William out of the blue report something very similar to me really said something to me, and I did not like it.

I know what it's like to be confronted by predatory animals in this place where I spend so much time, including a bit of a mountain lion encounter once. I know what that feels like.

This had nothing to do with that.

I don't think I can stress that enough.

In such a state, we waited out the night. Even though we'd meant to stay another day and night...we both decided although we obviously can't leave right now, we're going to get up in the morning, we're going to do all the work, we're going to get out before nightfall tomorrow, and we're going to get the hell out of here.

It seemed fine in the daylight, so that was what we did. Spent the next day chopping wood. That gave us about three hours to get out. I barely missed my mark. I had intended to have us out before dark. On this five-mile trail I got us to within a quarter mile of the parking lot. The moon comes up, just below the trail's steepest section. Right at nightfall with the full moon cresting over the mountains, to our east. And right then, a quarter mile away from the end, we hear this absolutely freakish fucking blood curdling scream. Something like an extremely angry nonhuman primate. Like a chimpanzee just flipping the fuck out.

This prompted us to get large sticks and instead of just facing forward, kind of sweeping our lights in arcs around the forest for that last quarter mile.

The whole trip had been a deliberate midweek thing. I had

intentionally gone at a time when no one else was around. When I go to the wilderness, I tend to go for the solitude of it, and this was no exception. Almost no one makes it as far as the cabin, but we saw no one on the trail, even on some of the loop sections where people tend to go, like out to see all the redwood groves and then back to the parking lot.

We finished up that last quarter mile about as fast as we could.

There was one car in the parking lot full of young people, college student age. We decided it was likely them yelling something across the canyon and that the distortion caused it to sound the way we heard it. It was probably the acoustics of the canyon itself. I don't know what they were doing there. They hadn't been on the trail, at least not while we were on it.

That was it for that adventure. Sort of. The physical part. We got in the truck, went home. In the morning I remembered something I had not thought of for a very long time. I had brushed it off when it happened as not very meaningful. As a kid I had some sleep paralysis incidents. God, is that a thing. Spent a long time wondering what the fuck that was until later in life I encountered other people discussing it.

About 2017 my daughter Kayla used to work on the R—— Cave project with me. I was out in the yard. I usually get up pretty early, get the water boiling, the coffee going, get everybody going, start planning for the day. While I am outside Kayla comes out, kind of visibly shaken.

She tells me this story. It didn't affect me too much at the time, in terms of the way this recent experience at the cabin did. I told her I know exactly what it is. I've had it before, it's cool, you don't need to be afraid of it.

So she told me. She was just, you know, really freaked out. She said I woke up. I looked out the window. There was something hanging in the tree looking at me. It was hanging between two trees. It was white, it was hairless, and its arms were too long, about double-length and bending the wrong way. Its eyes were almost like not there. Like they were hollow. Like not the orb of an eye, or hollow, like eyeless eye sockets. But like a nothing darkness. It just kept watching her, kind of moving its head.

I was like wow, yeah, I mean, I remember when something sort of like that stood over the foot of my bed and stuck its hand straight through my chest and grabbed my heart. Which of course didn't actually happen, but go, sleep paralysis! I was extremely confident that's what it was.

But after the experience that William and I had, it got pretty weird.

Having remembered this story, I went back to Kayla, and said if you're okay doing it, please retell that story, about the thing you saw when you came out and talked to me. It kind of caught her off guard, but she did tell the story, and it was exactly as I remembered it and exactly as I'm relating it to you.

But the thing she added was that she was wide awake and looking out the window, and she was perfectly able to move. It was in no way like sleep paralysis.

There's one last piece that goes with that. After I talked to Kayla, William talked to Cassie. Cassie came and talked to me about it. Kayla had never told her story to William or Cassie. Nor had I ever discussed it with William, nor had I ever discussed it with Kayla again. There hadn't really been any recounting of it since it happened, until I'd asked her this day. Cassie didn't have that piece of information when she came to me to tell me what William had said.

When William got home, he had kind of debriefed her on the whole thing. He added a detail. He had thought the whole experience was really great. Except the night, which was pretty horrific. Basically, he had the same experience I did. He was embarrassed and didn't want to let on to me about it. His version to me was that something was really wrong, and he was about to go out and ask me come in. The version he told Cassie, was, just before...let me back up...

While he was in cabin, I was in-cave for about an hour and a quarter on a solo water trip. While I was gone, he was apparently just really uncomfortable. He had a feeling something was really, really wrong. Really off. I called him from the cave phone, from the east stream where the water collection site is. When I made contact with him from inside the cave, that was when I first detected something was wrong, but I didn't know what it was. He was doing this mmmhmmm mmmhmmm thing. It sounded like he was frustrated. It turns out this is something he does when he's very nervous, though I didn't understand that at the time.

What he described to Cassie was different, or, if not different, carrying additional detail that he hadn't told me. There is a window in the cabin that faces east, and the way he described it to Cassie was that he looked at that window once and saw nothing, but that he couldn't look at it again.

He knew something was wrong, and he knew it was watching him, so he just looked away from it all the time. But he knew what it looked like, and it was pretty much like what Kayla saw. Like something almost human, and something like the Gollum creature from *Lord of the Rings*, but with different, dark eyes, and limbs bent all wrong.

The weirdest weirdness to me is weirdness that can affect people in the same way. Anti-cholinergic, people see spiders. Benadryl, scopolamine, atropine. Why is there a common experience behind that?

Greg finished his story before we reached Mariposa. We decided to stop there for dinner at Don Ruben's, which has been my preferred restaurant there ever since some work several colleagues and I did at the local museum a few years ago, creating 3D images of baskets made by Indigenous California basketweavers. Although we didn't discuss Greg's story much over dinner—he had told it so straightforwardly and thoroughly that there was little need to—I now shared the burden of his knowledge, if acquired secondhand, and I now had to consider whether I really wanted to spend the night in some lonely part of the Sierras. But if Greg could carry on, so could I.

From Mariposa, we began our ascent out of the foothills and into the Sierras proper. Very quickly, we found ourselves gaining elevation rapidly on winding dirt roads where ours was the only vehicle. Sometimes the road rose over ridges with no live trees in sight. The higher we climbed, the more obvious became the ravages of drought, beetles, and fire.

It soon became obvious that our enjoyable dinner had

probably cost us any chances of setting up camp in the dark. As we are both cavers, and well-equipped with lights as well as experienced in showing up at camp at 1:00 a.m. and pitching our tents in the dark, we saw this as a minor inconvenience at most. In that regard at least, the dark was not an obstacle.

Eventually we reached a height where we had a clear and spectacular view to the west, with the evening star hanging in the upper reaches of a flat, impoverished rainbow that the sunset spread across the horizon, shading directly from orange into blue with no more than a hint of yellow in between. Only a few bare spires remained of the forest here. We stopped to take a few photos of that awesome and desolate vista, standing on the bed and cab of Greg's truck.

Night fell quickly from that point onward, and we soon found ourselves in deeper forest again. The road constricted to a two-track. Fortunately, the Forest Service must have graded it since the rain stopped falling several months back. We repeatedly passed through the chainsawed gaps in large tree trunks that had fallen across the road, in some places barely wide enough for the truck to pass.

The road leveled at times and even dipped briefly, but the overall trend was always upward. After a while the road began to wind along a ridge top, and we could see an isolated point of light above us at the high end of a saddle to the north. We knew this had to be the fire lookout at Devil's Peak. I pictured a lone fire watcher up there, eating beans out of a can warmed over a Sterno while reading a dog-eared copy of Kerouac's *Desolations Angels*. I could not imagine they would be excited by our arrival. By this time we were driving in almost complete darkness.

This presented a serious problem. Although we had not seen another vehicle for miles, the road had long since narrowed so much that if we were to encounter someone coming from the opposite direction, one or both vehicles would have to back up. With a steep drop of a hundred meters or more on our left, this would be a sketchy operation at any time, but the darkness complicated the danger beyond any reasonable risk. We accepted that we were not going to reach Devil's Peak, which was still several miles away. We began to look for a turnout where we could pull off and camp. Anywhere off the road.

We got lucky pretty quickly. The road dipped slightly and forked, but just where it divided we saw a large clearing on our right. Beyond the clearing three roads led off. The main track led down and onward to the north. Another road led upward, a dark tunnel into denser forest, ostensibly toward the lookout on Devil's Peak. The third cut sharply to the right and downward, away to the east. Several massive pine trunks blocked the main track, all untouched by forest service saws. The downed trees were so tangled that I thought immediately of the twisted bridge girders in *The Evil Dead*. Despite this ominous association, we decided immediately that this clearing would be our home for the night. Greg parked the truck and we set up our tents.

The clearing was a wide oval perhaps 50 meters along its north-south axis. It occupied a small saddle, with both the north and south ends rising slightly. A steep slope dropped off to our west, and with our headlamps, we could see below us the bare trunks of trees burned in a forest fire at least several years back. East of the clearing rose a lush deciduous forest. This oasis, seemingly free of damage from either fire or the beetle-borne diseases that have stricken the trees of the Sierra Nevadas, struck us both as unusual. The clearing itself was a flat dirt surface, lacking any vegetation and almost without rocks, which made it an almost ideal campsite. We surmised that the Forest Service had cleared it with a bulldozer, presumably as some kind of staging area for fire-fighting equipment, perhaps even as a helicopter refueling station. We could see the tire tracks of other vehicles in the fine, dry soil, but not the marks of heavy machinery. Given the visibility our campsite afforded, we felt we had chosen an optimal spot to watch for the Nightwalkers.

After setting up our tents, which didn't take long, we began our vigil. As we sat on the tailgate of Greg's truck and scanned the clearing and slopes beyond, alternatively with and without our headlamps, we talked, covering a range of topics similar to our dinner conversation. More than once, we lapsed naturally into silence for minutes at a time. During one of these silent stretches, I became fully conscious of something even stranger than the untouched oasis on the east side of the clearing. I turned to Greg and asked him have you ever been anywhere so quiet, other than the deep interior of a cave?

The whole time we had been there, we had heard almost no sounds we did not make ourselves. Early on we heard a stick break off to our east, and we listened attentively for several minutes to ensure that neither large animal nor fellow human was approaching, but we heard nothing more. The whole night we did not hear any birds or small animals, with the sole exception of a single bat that flew across the clearing occasionally, and twice uttered a faint squeak. Outside of that bat, we saw no living things in the clearing other than a few tiny moths and a thin stream of ants. Greg confirmed that he had never experienced such near-absolute silence during all his previous time in the Sierras.

We seemed to have chosen some kind of dead zone for our camp, a realization that became even more disconcerting in light of Greg's recent experience elsewhere in the Sierras only two nights earlier. We compared and discussed our impressions. Neither of us felt even a twinge of trepidation, let alone the sort of overwhelming compulsion that had driven Greg from his hammock and into the cabin in L—— Canyon. To me the feeling was almost peaceful, though not soothing. I experienced no sense of any presence, whether benevolent or malign. What we felt was more of an absence or emptiness than anything else. We resolved to continue our vigil, but to remain on alert for anything untoward, other than the Nightwalkers themselves, whose possible arrival we were now considering more seriously than ever before. We agreed that if anything went the leastways pear-shaped, we would hop in the truck and hightail it back down the mountain without hesitation, leaving our tents and sleeping bags behind.

We continued our vigil, though somewhat more subdued. We both had the constant feeling that whole herds of Fresno Nightwalkers were marching across the clearing whenever and wherever our backs were turned. We were fully prepared to see them by this point. To encounter them, and only them, rather than something unexpected, would have been a relief. We periodically turned and swept all parts of the clearing with our lights.

At one point, we got up from the truck and walked some distance down the east road. As soon as we left the clearing, we saw spiders and insects (mostly beetles—Carabidae, Cantharidae, Cerambicidae, and Tenebrionidae—but also more moths), as well as a wide variety of trees and smaller plants, some with flowers. In one place I found a fragment of pressure-flaked obsidian, the remnant of some tool once used by the Miwok, or perhaps some even older group ancestral to them. We walked far enough that we could see the lights of Mariposa and other communities in the valley below. Then we returned to the clearing and resumed our vigil. Around 2:00 a.m. we adjourned to our tents and went to sleep. In the morning I scanned the clearing for unusual footprints, but saw nothing but our own and the vehicle tracks that had been there on our arrival. We struck camp and headed home. Though neither of us could shake the feeling that battalions of the creatures had passed just behind our backs during every unobserved moment of the night, the question of the Fresno Nightwalkers' existence remains unresolved,

•

Events in the several months since Greg and I conducted our somewhat semi-serious stakeout require me to append a disturbing coda to this narrative. On August 15, Jonathan

Gerrish, Ellen Chung, their 1-year-old daughter, Aurelia Miju Chung-Gerrish, and their family dog, Oski all died while on a hiking trip in the Sierra Nevadas. A search team found their bodies two days later in Devil's Gulch, about five miles from where Greg and I had camped less than two months earlier. Here in the Central Valley and the eastern Foothills, the tragic fate of this family has been steadily in the news ever since, and the story has made national, if not international headlines as well. Some readers will probably recall it. I am typing these words the day after Mariposa County Sheriff Jeremy Briese finally announced the official cause of death for the family as hyperthermia and "probable dehydration." Heat stroke. Briese acknowledged that Oski's death remains unexplained.

In the intervening months, medical examiners had already ruled out many other possibilities as the cause of death, including gunshot, ingestion of anatoxin-a from a toxic algae bloom in the Merced River, and exposure to poisonous gas from abandoned mines. In September, the Bureau of Land Management and the Forest Service closed off areas of the forest surrounding and including Devil's Gulch, citing "unknown hazards found in and near the Savage Lundy Trail." Those closures remain in effect, the hazards unidentified.

Although I have no idea what caused these tragic deaths, Sheriff Briese's official explanation feels unsatisfactory. I will leave conspiracy theorizing and wild speculations to others. I am sure all that is coming on its own. This case has the potential to become North America's equivalent of the tragic 1959 Dyatlov Pass incident ("гибель тургруппы

Дятлова," which literally translated, means "The Dyatlov Group Demise"), in which nine experienced Russian hikers from the Ural Polytechnical Institute died from unexplained causes on the eastern slope of Kholat Syakhl, whose name in the Indigenous Mansi language means "Dead Mountain." The most recent official explanation attributes the deaths to an avalanche, which killed some of the team members and forced the others to leave their damaged tents without adequate clothing, but various accounts have also claimed that the bodies of at least some of the hikers were badly mutilated, torn apart from the inside, or even radioactive. Secret military experiments and UFOs have frequently received blame. I expect we will soon see similar "explanations" bandied about for the deaths of the Chung-Gerrish family.

Neither Greg nor I was aware of the place name "Devil's Gulch" when we planned our trip. It had not appeared when we searched for a promising location. We chose Devil's Peak because it was the most prominent feature labeled at the lowest resolution/highest level map view of the terrain. If we had known of the somewhat more accessible Devil's Gulch, we almost certainly would have chosen it instead for our vigil. Neither of us plan to visit Devil's Gulch if and when the Forest Service lifts its restrictions on the area. Or any time afterward. Nor do we plan to return to that desolate clearing near Devil's Peak where we spent the night of June 24, 2021. If the Fresno Nightcrawler walks there, let it walk alone.

The research station was destroyed by the KNP Fire sometime on or around October 4.

Scott Nicolay is an archaeologist and caver specializing in prehistoric cave use and iconography in the North American Southwest/Northwest Mexico, Mesoamerica, and Island Oceania. His story "Do You Like to Look at Monsters" won the World Fantasy Award for Best Short Fiction in 2015. He is currently translating and editing the fiction of Belgian weird fiction author Jean Ray and editing the posthumous publication of works by American author John D. Keefauver.

Ruiz and the Echo Hotel

Nick Walker

Special Agent Margarita Ruiz is undercover tonight, wearing cheap grungy spacer clothes, hunched over a pint of beer in the darkest corner of the most disreputable barroom in the Cordova Spaceport Complex, all because the Reality Patrol got word that the notorious interdimensional space pirate Rissa Flammarion will be putting in an appearance. The beer's just a prop, no way she's drinking that shit, it smells rancid as fuck. She's in a foul mood, and she needs to take a piss, and she has no idea she's going to fall in love.

Her partner on this mission, Agent Smiley, isn't drinking either, but he's doing a good job of faking it: one foot up on the table, bottle in hand, gesticulating his way through some wild rambling tale he's probably making up as he goes. Smiley's a specialist in undercover work, and a firm believer in the principle that the best way to avoid attracting too much attention is to act like you don't mind attention at all.

They make a good team, but Ruiz doesn't share Smiley's enthusiasm for subterfuge. She does better with those assignments where she can go full Woman-in-Black, rocking the regulation suit and trenchcoat and dark glasses. Flash a gun and a badge, take charge, sort shit out. Not that she's any kind of fascist, or at least she sure as hell hopes she isn't. She just prefers things straightforward, is all, and she especially prefers not having to sit all night trying to ignore her full bladder in a spaceport bar packed with sweaty lowlifes.

About this bladder situation: Truth be told, Ruiz is big-time squeamish when it comes to public toilets. She's one of those people to whom cleanliness matters enough that even now, more than two decades later, the shit-spattered bathrooms she had to use in junior high school still feature prominently in her nightmares. And this filthy dive she's got the misfortune to be in tonight, well, there's a puddle of puke on the floor over there that no one's bothered to mop up, and the sleeve of her flight jacket keeps getting stuck to the table, so she shudders at the thought of what the restroom amenities here must be like. But she's put it off as long as she can, and now she's at the squirming-and-squeezing-her-legs-together stage, which is going to be a problem if their target shows up. Only thing worse than using the toilet in this foul establishment would be peeing her pants in the middle of trying to bust Rissa Flammarion, with whom Ruiz already has a bit of an embarrassing history.

So at last she mumbles something to Smiley about finding the facilities, and he gives her a sympathetic look and wishes her best of luck, and she's off on her quest for relief. At least half the patrons are smoking one thing or another, and the noxious fog that passes for air in here is damn near opaque. Squinting through the haze, she weaves her way among tables and chairs and drunken goons, doing her best to avoid getting jostled, till she spots a promising archway in a far corner. But alas, this only leads her into a maze of semi-partitioned seating and gambling areas, even smokier and more crowded than the main barroom and laid out in no evident pattern. Between the baffling floor plan, the dim lighting, the fuliginous atmosphere, and the absence of legible signage, the location of the restroom remains elusive.

By the time she spies the gray plastic door, tucked away in the shadows of some obscure alcove, she's in serious distress. The door's got a little symbol stenciled on it that looks like a teardrop, which probably means water, and which she very much hopes is meant to indicate the presence of toilets and not an indoor pond full of alligators or some such thing. In a place like this, you never know.

Standing next to the door is a woman who looks so entirely foreign to this environment that even in her present state of urgency, Ruiz can't help but take notice. Tall and pale and thin, long ash-blonde hair, festooned in a riot of multicolored scarves over an iridescent blouse and ankle-length skirt, she's got the vibe of some eccentric librarian character from a children's TV show, the kind of person who'd own a magic storybook. She's gazing at her surroundings with eager curiosity, like this wretched den of two-bit interplanetary thugs is an enchanted forest and she's hoping to spot a unicorn.

Why's this strange person so familiar? Doesn't click till the woman turns her head, revealing a string of tattooed hieroglyphs that begins at her left temple and winds its way down the side of her face and neck. Then Ruiz remembers: a briefing, months ago, multiple slides of this attractive tattooed face from various angles, amidst shots of other persons of interest. This is none other than Madeline Erzsebet de Verninac, of the Order of Eight Directions.

The Reality Patrol officially classifies the Order of Eight Directions as an interdimensional terrorist organization. Far as Ruiz has been able to tell, though, it's neither terroristic nor organized. More like a loose-knit assortment of interdimensional explorers, vagabonds, smugglers, scholars, thieves, pranksters, crackpots, gonzo journalists, and hedonistic thrill-seekers. This de Verninac sure as hell doesn't look like she's about to terrorize anyone. As best Ruiz can recall from that briefing, de Verninac's ventures into interdimensional crime have largely consisted of pilfering rare manuscripts and trafficking in Secrets Man Was Not Meant to Know. Small-time stuff compared with the misdeeds of Rissa Flammarion, the target of tonight's mission, who once destroyed an entire planet in order to win a bar bet.

So for a second or two Ruiz considers ignoring de Verninac and continuing right through that gray plastic door. But then she remembers that Flammarion and the Order of Eight Directions, much as they might differ from one another when it comes to motives and body count, have been known to work together when their interests align—making the presence of a member of the Order, in this particular obscure spaceport bar on this particular night, unlikely to be mere coincidence.

The smart play here would be to apprehend de Verninac on the spot. Get up close, jam a pistol into her ribs, intimidate her into revealing what she knows about the deal going down tonight. But Ruiz desperately needs to get to that restroom. Problem is, if she hits the restroom first, there's no guarantee de Verninac will still be standing here when she gets back. And if she makes a move on de Verninac *before* hitting the restroom? *Then* what? Question her and rush off to pee afterward, leaving the blasted woman free to warn Flammarion? No, once she reveals herself to de Verninac, Ruiz will have to take her into custody, keep her at gunpoint until the mission wraps up. And how the hell do you hold someone at gunpoint while using the toilet? Bring her into the stall with you? Seems more than a little awkward.

She's getting closer and closer to de Verninac and the door, and to the point where she'll have to choose between them. She tries to keep her face neutral, play it cool, because de Verninac is watching her now and making no secret of it. Gawking openly, in fact, in a way that makes Ruiz wonder if she's high on something. And then, when Ruiz is just a few paces away, de Verninac looks right into her eyes, flashes an impish little smile, and in a quick smooth motion opens the door herself and vanishes into whatever space lies beyond. The door swings shut behind her.

Fuck. Ruiz lunges after her, drawing the pistol from

under her jacket as she shoves the door open again and finds not a restroom, goddammit, but a junction of narrow gray-walled maintenance corridors lined with pipes and cables and ductwork. She catches a glimpse of one of de Verninac's colorful scarves as its owner disappears around a bend, and the chase is on. Sprinting through a maze of twisty little passages, boots pounding the floor. Her full bladder is agony, thank fuck she's been doing her kegels. De Verninac's fast on those long legs but Ruiz stays on her tail, skidding around each corner just in time to see which corner her quarry turns next.

This labyrinth of maintenance corridors seems more extensive than even a sprawling spaceport ought to need, and things are starting to look a bit odd. Metal walls have given way to cement, then to smooth plaster painted in robin's-egg blue, and who the hell paints a maintenance corridor robin's-egg blue? Are these even maintenance corridors anymore? The steel pipes and ductwork petered out a few twists and turns ago. And just as all this is occurring to her, she rounds one last corner and sees a final stretch of blue-walled hallway that ends in a wooden door. Nowhere else de Verninac could've gone. Knob turns easily and Ruiz charges through the doorway, brandishing her pistol.

And finds herself in what appears to be a cozy little café, fancy décor, nice wood paneling, bit of a 1920s art deco sort of vibe, rich smell of coffee in the air, a few small round tables with comfy-looking chairs. De Verninac is seated at one of the tables, legs crossed and hands folded demurely in her lap, with that mischievous smile on her face. Doesn't seem to even be breathing hard, much less panting and sweating the way Ruiz is after that wild chase. There's no one else in sight. No windows, either, but Ruiz doesn't need to look outside to know she's not in the same universe as the Cordova Spaceport Complex anymore.

Travel between universes is generally accomplished via some form of portal. There are other ways, though— including the phenomenon known as *straying*, in which a person wandering in strange territory passes by accident into some liminal zone outside their accustomed reality, and thence into a different reality altogether. A propensity for straying is one of the more troublesome symptoms of the metaphysical disorder that the Reality Patrol refers to as Chronic Synchronicity Syndrome and most folks just call Weird Luck. Weird Luck is a prerequisite for membership in the Order of Eight Directions, and certain members of the Order have mastered the esoteric skill of straying *on purpose*, to destinations of their own choosing. It just so happens that Ruiz herself has been diagnosed with Chronic Synchronicity Syndrome, by the specialists in the Reality Patrol's Department of Ontological Medicine, and although hers is a relatively mild case and she's never strayed on her own, this isn't the first time it's rendered her susceptible to inadvertently following a member of the Order of Eight Directions out of one reality and into another.

She stands there pointing her pistol at de Verninac, trying to catch her breath and hold her pee in at the same time, wondering what the hell to do. And then de Verninac, whose infuriating smile hasn't wavered and who appears entirely unperturbed by the pistol, gestures toward a door

in a far corner of the room and says, "If you need the restroom, it's right over there."

For a moment Ruiz is frozen, unable to get her brain in
gear to make a decision.

"Come on, silly. I could've escaped if I wanted. Go and pee.
I promise I'll wait."

Urinary desperation wins out, and Ruiz makes a dash
for that door. Yanks it open, and praise all the gods, finds
not just a restroom but a *nice* restroom. Immaculate. Kind
of restroom you'd find in the home of some well-to-do personage possessed of excellent taste and an obsession with
absolute cleanliness. She gets her pants undone and makes
it onto that toilet just in time, and nearly weeps with relief
as she has the best and longest piss of her life.

Besides Weird Luck, the one thing all members of the
Order of Eight Directions have in common is their ability
to access the Archive. Depending who you ask, the Archive
is either a vast library which has somehow been turned
into a separate universe all its own, or a separate universe
which has been turned into a library. There are numerous
small pocket universes of this sort woven into the fabric
of the multiverse, but the Archive's one of the few that are
known to be self-aware. No one finds the Archive unless
the Archive wants them to, which is why the Reality Patrol,
despite its incomparable resources, has never been able to
raid the place.

So Ruiz's first question, now that she can concentrate on
something other than holding her pee in, is whether this
place is part of the Archive. She washes her hands, splash-
es some cold water on her face, gives her reflection in the

mirror a look that says *What the fuck have you got me into this time*, and exits the restroom to find de Verninac waiting for her as promised. Still no sign of anyone else, but somehow the table's now been set with a couple of china cups and saucers, and a fancy little teapot with steam rising merrily from the spout. Ruiz plops herself down in the chair across from de Verninac, folds her arms, and comes right to the point: "Is this the Archive?"

"The Archive? Oh, no. The Archive was never this nice. Tea?"

"Where the fuck am I, then?"

De Verninac doesn't seem any more bothered by Ruiz's surly tone than she was by the pistol. "You're in the Echo Hotel. Another pocket universe. Not nearly as well-known as the Archive, but she *is* self-aware."

"You led me here. Why?"

"You looked like someone it would be fun to meet, so I decided to see if you'd follow me. And you did! Just like Alice, chasing the White Rabbit, pitter-pat, down the hole to Wonderland. And now we can have a tea party! Just like Alice. You *will* have some tea, won't you?"

Ruiz can't tell if this *chica* is a genuine screwball or just screwing with her, but it seems like her best shot at getting more information is to play along for now. So she says, "Sure, tea, why not," and de Verninac's face lights up even brighter. It really is a striking face, some fine bone structure going on there, eyes the same emerald green as those intricate little tattoos. Ruiz watches her pour the tea, then says, "Just so we're clear... you do understand I'm a Reality Patrol agent, right?"

"Are you? What's that like? I want to hear all about it."

"No, I mean... Look, you're an interdimensional criminal. A terrorist, far as the Reality Patrol's concerned."

"How exciting! You make me sound so dangerous!"

Nothing about this conversation is going the way Ruiz expects, but she presses on. "I'm saying I could arrest you right now. Haul your allegedly terroristic ass off to a Reality Patrol base where they'd interrogate you for months. But we don't have to do it that way. It's Flammarion I'm after. Give me any info that can help us take her down, and we can keep this a friendly little tea party."

"Oh, you can't arrest anyone *here*. The Echo Hotel would *never* allow anyone to be taken from the premises against their will. And anyway, I've no idea what mischief Rissa might be up to. I haven't seen her in quite some time."

"What were you doing in that bar, then? Weird Luck or not, no way it's a coincidence that of all the gin joints in all the spaceports in all the multiverse, you walked into the one where she's got a deal going down."

"Ooh, is this what it's like to be interrogated? I like it! You're right, it was no coincidence. One never knows where Rissa's going to show up next, but this time a rumor's leaked out. I heard it from a guest here, and I thought, I could do with a bit of excitement, maybe I'll drop by and say hi to her. Then I got to the place and saw *you*, and I just had the best feeling about you. I could tell getting to know you would be ever so much more interesting than a reunion with Rissa."

"And you decided the way to get to know me was to run away from me so that I'd chase you into another universe which is apparently a self-aware hotel."

"Yes! Wasn't that ever so *naughty* of me?"

Ruiz sighs and stands up. "Know what? I believe you. It's so ridiculous, it's gotta be true. If you were lying, you'd've come up with something better. So have a nice tea party, I guess. I got a mission to get back to." The door she originally came in through isn't open anymore, though she doesn't remember closing it. She goes over, opens it, and instead of the expected hallway finds a tidy little closet, shelves stocked with an assortment of puzzles and board games. Fuck. She turns to glare at de Verninac, who's watching with undisguised amusement. "Seriously? I don't have time for this shit. How the fuck do I get out of here?"

De Verninac takes a dainty sip of tea. "Oh, no need to worry about *time*. Whenever you're ready to return to your mission, just stand in front of any door and tell the hotel where you want the door to lead, and what time you want to arrive there. You can't go further back in time than the moment when you entered the hotel, but you could stay here for *weeks*, or *months* even, and still reappear in that bar just a few seconds after the point when you left it."

"Hunh. Nice." Ruiz shuts the door again, stands facing it, then glances back over her shoulder. "So, what, I just talk out loud and the hotel will hear me?"

"Yes, but wait! Please? You don't have to leave right away! You haven't even *touched* your tea!"

"Yeah, no offense, but that tea could be dosed with damn near anything. Last thing I need is to get back to that bar and discover I'm tripping my face off in the middle of a mission. So, uh, this has been an interesting little detour and all, but I got no reason to stick around here."

"But I led you on that whole big chase! I could tell you had to pee really bad, too." That impish smile is back again.

"Yeah, you're a huge pain in the ass. But you did find me a restroom that was actually *clean*, so let's call it even."

"But it must have been so uncomfortable! You should've seen your face when you got here. You were furious! Bet it was embarrassing, too, when you had to run for the toilet." De Verninac giggles. "I've just been so terribly naughty, haven't I? I'm not the least bit repentant, either."

"Yeah, sure, whatever. You're the absolute worst, if that makes you happy. Not sure what you want from me, here."

"Well, Miss Reality Patrol Agent, you've caught me, and aren't you supposed to make sure justice is done?" De Verninac's smile turns positively devilish. "Doesn't a naughty girl like me deserve to be thoroughly punished?"

Oh.

Oh, *shit*.

That's what this is about.

Ruiz has never been good at the whole flirtation thing. Fails to pick up on the subtle cues. What cues did she miss this time, before de Verninac abandoned subtlety altogether?

And what the hell does she do *now*?

•

What she does, in the end, is she goes for it.

There are a zillion reasons why jumping into bed with this possibly insane interdimensional criminal is terrible idea, but fuck it. Ruiz has always had a thing for weird kinky geek chicks, and that smile and the unabashedly porn-worthy line about deserving to be punished are an irresistible combo. And how often in one lifetime does an opportunity like this come along?

She strides over to de Verninac, offers a hand, and pulls her to her feet. For a brief moment they stand face to face, and then they're all over each other, tongues in each other's mouths, hands in each other's hair. And holy shit this de Verninac is a wildcat, and goddamn she smells amazing. Then she breaks away, grinning, says, "Catch me!" and darts out through a small open doorway Ruiz could've sworn wasn't there a minute ago. Which leads, it turns out, to an enormous marble-floored hotel lobby with a fountain at its center, a museum's worth of art on the walls, and a lot of armchairs and couches upholstered in brown leather. No one else here, not even a front desk clerk, and like the café it's windowless and impeccably maintained. There's an atmosphere of tasteful majesty which is apparently lost on de Verninac, who shrieks with delight as she scampers over any piece of furniture in her path. Ruiz stays on her tail all the way across the room, and then up two long curving flights of wide marble stairs. Good thing the Reality Patrol requires its field agents to stay in shape, because de Verninac seems tireless.

They're running down a broad hallway, past a series of numbered doors, when de Verninac suddenly pivots midstride, opens a door, and dives into a room. Ruiz plunges after her and finds herself in the most posh hotel suite she's ever seen. De Verninac is sitting on the edge of the massive four-poster bed, grinning a Cheshire Cat grin. Ruiz kicks the door shut behind her and charges headlong, barreling into de Verninac and landing on top of her.

A ferocious tussle ensues, during which Ruiz gradually succeeds in divesting de Verninac of her various multicolored scarves, followed by her blouse, shoes, skirt, and underclothes. De Verninac squeals in gleeful mock-protest at the loss of each item, then squirms theatrically as Ruiz uses those scarves to secure her wrists and ankles to the bedposts. "Are you sure this is standard Reality Patrol procedure?" she says, as Ruiz ties the final knot.

"It's within acceptable mission parameters," Ruiz assures her. "Especially when apprehending a very naughty suspect who's shown herself to be a flight risk." She examines her prisoner. That string of exquisite little tattooed hieroglyphs on the side of de Verninac's face continues all the way down her torso, it turns out, and spirals around her slender left leg like a vine. "Now then, I believe you said something about deserving to be punished?"

•

By the time she decides this impudent wench has been sufficiently tamed and can be untied at least temporarily, Ruiz is thinking of her as *Madeline* rather than *de Verninac*. Once someone's let you tie them up in bed, she figures, you should assume you're on a first-name basis.

They're laying side-by-side on the bed, occasionally kissing, when Ruiz says, "This has been fun, babe, but I'm starving. Afraid I'm gonna have to eat you now."

"Please, Miss Ravening Monster," Madeline says, "if only you'll spare me, I'll reveal to you one of the great secrets of the cosmos."

Ruiz rolls on top of her, pinning her down. "Tell me the secret, little morsel, and I'll decide whether to spare you."

"Eek! The secret is that the Echo Hotel has the best room service in the multiverse."

"Mmm. That *is* a good secret. I'll spare you for now, but I might decide to eat you later for dessert."

She picks up the receiver of the antique telephone on the nightstand, which has neither buttons nor dial, and a cheerful voice on the other end of the line says, "Room service."

"Yeah, can we get dinner for two?"

"Certainly. What will you be having?"

"Uh, what's on the menu tonight?"

"Anything you'd like."

"Yeah, but, I mean... what are my choices?"

"It will be my pleasure to prepare any food you can name."

"Hang on, I'll call back."

Ruiz hangs up and turns to Madeline, who's still pinned beneath her. "They say we can order *anything*."

"I *told* you it was the best."

So after a brief discussion in which Madeline claims to be up for whatever Ruiz wants, Ruiz picks up the phone again and orders crab rangoon, mu shu pork, prawn lo mein, and a chocolate cake. A surprisingly short time later, couldn't be more than five minutes, there's a knock at the door. She throws on one of the bathrobes she finds hanging in the closet, and peeks out into the hallway. No one in sight, but there's a cart waiting there with a bunch of covered platters on it containing everything she ordered. It's one of the best meals she's ever had.

Next time they order room service—after a shower, more sex, a long nap, an epic pillow fight, and a luxurious soak in the suite's hot tub—Ruiz gets curious and waits outside the door of the suite to see if the cart of food is delivered by an actual person, or if it just appears out of thin air. Pretty soon the cart comes rolling down the hall, pushed by a perky young woman in an immaculate red uniform.

"Good morning, ma'am," the woman says. "Here's your order. Anything else I can do for you?"

"Wait, it's morning already?"

"Well, there's no morning or evening in the Echo Hotel, ma'am, but it's always morning *somewhere*."

"Can't argue with *that*." Ruiz takes hold of the cart, starts to wheel it into the room. "Be right back out," she says. "Just gotta grab my wallet."

"No need, ma'am. The hospitality here is free of charge. Your presence, for as long as you choose to stay, is payment enough."

"Hunh. Well, *that's* cool. But I at least oughta tip you."

The woman laughs. "Oh, no, ma'am, I don't need money. I'm an echo."

"A what?"

"I'm the Echo Hotel, ma'am. I create these bodies and play them like characters in a theatrical production, to interact with my guests in a human sort of way. I call them echoes because I base them on guests who've visited me in the past, so they're like echoes of the originals. This one's based on a member of a troupe of traveling performers who strayed into my corridors long ago, and ended up finding their way back to me for many a return visit."

Ruiz stands there and blinks at the woman a few times, trying to process all this. "Okay, hold on. You were created by the hotel?"

"Oh, no, ma'am. I *am* the hotel. This body has no mind separate from my own; it's part of me just like the walls and furnishings and air. I could just as easily speak to you as a disembodied voice coming from everywhere, but most guests find that sort of thing alarming. This way is so much more hospitable. And playing these characters is so *fun*."

Ruiz tries to wrap her brain around this, but her brain's like, *Nope, can't deal, weirdness overload, need time to process*. She stammers out some thanks to the woman-who-is-apparently-also-the-hotel, and retreats back into the suite. The woman-who-is-apparently-also-the-hotel has to remind her to bring the food cart in with her.

She rolls the cart into the suite's dining area. Madeline joins her, wrapped in one of those hotel bathrobes, and they dig into another magnificent feast—or rather, Madeline digs in, while Ruiz sits there and quietly freaks out until Madeline notices and asks what's troubling her. Ruiz does her best to explain how the woman from room service turned out to also be the actual hotel.

"An echo," Madeline says. "All the staff here are echoes. The hotel does them very well, don't you think?"

"I guess. it's just..."

"Something bothers you about it?"

"It's not the echo thing that bugs me. The *chica* from room service is part of the hotel? That much, I can deal with. I figure it's like being in a video game, right? The guests are players, and the staff, the echoes, they're like... non-player characters? Characters played by the computer."

"Mmm, that's a pretty good analogy."

"Except the hotel's not a computer, she's this whole reality. *That's* what's tripping me out here. I mean, you told me she was self-aware, but it didn't really sink in till I actually spoke with her. We're inside this giant self-aware being, whose body is basically made up of every molecule in this whole mini-universe. I mean, we're *breathing* her. That robe you're wearing is her. We've been *fucking* in her, on a bed that's *also* her. We've *peed* in her. And when we order food from room service, we're fucking *eating* her! Cause what else is there for her to make food out of, except atoms that are *part* of her?"

"But how is this different from the universe you originally came from? Or any other universe?"

"It's different cause the universe I came from wasn't a goddamn self-aware being!"

"Of course it was."

"Come on, seriously, how could you even know that?"

"*Every* universe is self-aware. Every universe is a living being whose body consists of all the energy within it, including the energy which manifests as matter."

"No way. Universe *I'm* from never fucking *talked* to me."

"Any sufficiently advanced mystic, in almost any culture in the history of any inhabited universe, would disagree with you on that point."

"No, but, I mean... Look, the Echo Hotel just fucking appeared to me as this totally flesh-and-blood woman, solid enough to push a food cart, and was like, 'Hey, I'm this universe you're in.' And now, what, I'm supposed to *eat* little pieces of her while she watches me from everywhere?"

"It occurs to me," Madeline says, "that maybe reactions like yours are precisely why most universes are more subtle about the ways they say hello. Are you religious?"

"Raised Catholic, but it didn't stick."

"I should think a Catholic upbringing would've left you well-accustomed to eating the body of an omnipresent being."

"Dammit, now you're just fucking with me."

"For which I should be severely punished. But first, consider this: almost every self-aware being has a deep-seated need to be *known*, to be experienced and recognized by a fellow consciousness. When the need goes unmet too long, we feel lonely. This is every bit as true for a universe, a cosmos, as it is for any other self-aware being. So what's a cosmos do when it gets lonely? It creates life within itself, and guides that life's evolution to produce self-aware beings like you. Beings who experience themselves as separate from the cosmos that created them, and who can thus meet the need of that cosmos to be experienced by consciousness other than its own."

"Holy shit," Ruiz says. "You're blowing my mind here."

"Hee! There's all *kinds* of ways I'd like to blow your mind. But we mustn't get distracted just yet; I was going somewhere with all this. These little pocket universes, like the Echo Hotel or the Archive? They don't have quite enough power to generate self-aware life. Sure, they can create puppets, like the echo-forms the hotel uses to give guests the experience of interacting with hotel staff. But a puppeteer alone with her puppets is still alone. Only way a pocket cosmos can meet its need to be known is if visitors from other universes find their way to her. And how does the Echo Hotel make sure she has no shortage of visitors? Same way any good hotel does: she treats each guest so well, they always want to come back."

"Wow. Put it *that* way, it's actually pretty fucking cool."

"I know, right? Anyway, my point is that eating or breathing or having sex in the Echo Hotel is no different from doing those things in any other universe, except the Echo Hotel's a lot more invested in your personal comfort than a bigger universe tends to be."

"Whoa, yeah, okay. Gonna be thinkin about this for a while, but it makes sense. It's just, now that I've had a conversation with her where she was acting all human and wearing a human-looking face, it's hard not to think of her as a person."

"Well, then, what if she *is* a person?" Madeline lifts the lid of the dessert tray on the room service cart, revealing half a dozen tiny chocolate brownies. Each one is covered in chocolate icing, with a perfect strawberry planted atop it. She picks up one of the strawberries between her thumb and forefinger, extends her long pink tongue, and proceeds to slowly lick the strawberry clean of icing. She's got Ruiz's full attention here. She takes her time. When she's licked that strawberry till it shines, she holds it up and studies it closely. "Yes," she says, "let's say the Echo Hotel is a person. Just another fun-loving lass like ourselves. Sure, this food is part of her. But are you seriously going to tell me that putting parts of another woman's body in your mouth can't be a lot of fun, when you know she's into it?" And with that, she opens her mouth, pops the strawberry inside, and grins at Ruiz as she chews and swallows.

Ruiz is briefly speechless. Madeline stands up and leans toward her across the small table. She maintains eye contact while she licks a bit of strawberry juice off one slender finger. "And as for the sex," she says, "well, it would be *such* a shame if you were too much of a prude to play with me while our fun-loving hostess watches."

Ruiz launches herself out of her chair and makes a grab for the little tease. Madeline twists out of the way and flees into the bedroom with Ruiz hot on her heels. She's slippery, but Ruiz is getting wise to her tricks by now and has her pinned down on the bed in less than a minute. "I'll show you who's a prude," Ruiz says, as she wrestles Madeline's bathrobe off. "You think I'm embarrassed to have the hotel watching? Why should *I* be embarrassed, when *you're* the one getting the bare-assed spanking?"

•

The Echo Hotel has no exterior. As Madeline explains it, the hotel comprises this whole universe, so to exit the hotel would mean leaving this universe for a different one—for instance, going back to that bar in the Cordova Spaceport Complex—or slipping outside of existence entirely, which Madeline doesn't recommend. The hotel's interior, meanwhile, proves far more extensive than Ruiz first imagined.

Thanks to Madeline's enthusiasm for being chased and captured, their games soon extend beyond the confines of their suite, and each excursion takes them into new territory. One day they come upon a full-size croquet lawn, real grass under a vast blue domed ceiling that does a pretty good job of looking like a real sky.

Madeline continues to be the most delightful playmate. Their games are endless variations on the pattern already established: Madeline teases and provokes, then there's the inevitable chase and struggle as she tries, or pretends to try, to escape the consequences. Ruiz captures her in the end, and metes out punishment until she promises she's learned her lesson. Then Madeline's a properly-tamed little pet for a while, but soon enough the cycle starts anew.

They never see another guest. Ruiz asks Madeline about this and learns that the hotel discreetly shuffles space, time, and architecture within herself to ensure that no guest runs into anyone they haven't consented to encounter. Ruiz immediately exploits this guarantee of privacy by declaring that Madeline's no longer allowed to wear clothes anywhere in the hotel. This makes their adventures outside the suite even more fun, plus Madeline's display of mock-indignation is priceless.

·

None of the electronic devices she carries on her person function at all in the Echo Hotel, and there's not a clock or a window to be found, so Ruiz ends up measuring the length of her stay by how many times she and Madeline order room service. She tells herself she'll stick around for a dozen meals, but ends up extending it to two dozen. That's where she has to draw the line, though.

"Why so soon?" Madeline wants to know, when Ruiz breaks the news during meal number twenty. "You can stay as long as you want and still return to that spaceport bar a minute after you left, remember? It'll be like no time's passed at all."

"Yeah, but time's passing for me *here*. Aside from the workout I get chasing down that spankable ass of yours, I'm not exactly keeping up my training regimen. I stay too long, I'll lose my edge. I mean, back at that bar, there's a mission in progress. If I go back to the mission and I've let myself get too far from peak condition, it could get me or my partner killed."

She expects Madeline to argue, or to try to tempt her into staying longer. But Madeline just looks at her with those big green eyes and says, "Will you please come back and visit me again soon?"

Ruiz was prepared for just about anything except this raw vulnerability. "I... uh..." She pauses. Takes a deep breath, and says, "Look, I really want to keep seeing you. Believe me, I don't want this to end. But I only got here by following you. I don't have a fucking clue how to find this place on my own. And even if I could get here, how do I know when *you'll* be here?"

And just like that, Madeline's all smiles again. "Oh, no need to worry about *that*," she says. "Now that you've been here, finding your way back on your own is easy. Weird Luck weaves its way and seeks its own. You just have to *let* it. Find someplace strange, someplace a bit on the labyrinthine side, and let yourself wander. And as you wander, just sort of daydream about the dear old Echo Hotel."

"You're talking about voluntary straying."

"Indeed I am. The secret to voluntary straying is there's not much of a secret. It's mostly a matter of Weird Luck, intentionality, and practice. Also, the hotel has ways of making herself easier to find, once she knows you and likes you. You even *start* to stray while thinking about her, she'll reach out and meet you more than halfway."

"I thought straying only happened to people whose Weird Luck was really severe."

"Look around you, hon. You tried to take a short trip to the restroom and somehow ended up making love to a suspected terrorist in a sentient extradimensional hotel. I think you might have a lot more potential for Weird Luck than you give yourself credit for. Oh, and anytime you can manage a visit is fine. More than fine, I mean. I'm here almost all the time, except when I've popped out to grab a book I need."

"I thought your usual base of operations was the Archive."

"Never! The Archive's hospitality is terrible. No room service at all. You get hungry in the Archive, you have to go get takeout food from another universe, or scrounge for leftovers. And don't even get me started on the state of the housekeeping. Sure, it's got more books—but there's a perfectly nice library *here*, too, and I'm always adding to it."

It occurs to Ruiz that when Madeline talks about popping out to grab a book, or adding more books to the hotel library, she's referring to the same activities that the Reality Patrol's files on her describe in less charitable terms as *an extensive series of interdimensional felonies involving the theft of rare and forbidden manuscripts, and the illegal transportation of said manuscripts across the borders of reality for nefarious purposes.* Oh, well. Far as Ruiz is concerned, Madeline's doing no real harm, no matter how sinister the official narrative makes her sound. Not that Ruiz would ever turn her in anyway, even if Madeline *were* up to something more nefarious than stocking a hotel library with weird books. Plenty of Reality Patrol agents who'd turn in a friend or lover for the sake of duty or to advance their careers, and find some way to rationalize it to themselves so they could go on feeling like one of the good guys. Ruiz, though, she promised herself a long time ago she'd never let this job turn her into *that* big an asshole.

On the other hand, now that it looks like Ruiz's upcoming departure won't have to be Goodbye Forever, Madeline's mention of her criminal activities seems like a perfect opportunity to steer the conversation in a more enjoyable direction. "So you confess to the crime of interdimensional book-stealing, do you? You realize, of course, that as a dedicated agent of the Reality Patrol, it's my duty to detain and punish you until you've learned the error of your ways."

Madeline springs to her feet. "You'll never take me alive!"

And once again, the chase is on.

•

Saying goodbye is hard, but Ruiz swears she'll find her way back as soon as she can. After a last long embrace, she stands in front of a randomly-chosen door in an alcove just off the hotel's lobby and says, "Uh, hey there, Echo Hotel. This satisfied customer is checking out now. Can you please make this door lead to that same shitty bar in the Cordova Spaceport Complex that I came here from, just a few seconds after I left?" She opens the door and finds the doorway filled with a smooth wall of shimmery iridescence. Standard interdimensional portal stuff, any experienced Reality Patrol field agent is well-accustomed to stepping through this kind of surface. So through it she steps—and just as advertised, she's back in the Spaceport Complex, at that junction of maintenance corridors where her first pursuit of Madeline began. The gray plastic door with the little teardrop symbol stenciled on it is right there beside her, and she pushes through it and back into the dim smoky bar. The stench of the place seems even worse now, after all that time breathing the sweet clean air of the hotel. She makes her way back to the main room and finds Agent Smiley sitting right where she left him.

•

According to the Reality Patrol's informant, Rissa Flammarion's coming to this bar to meet with an interdimensional smuggler named Palmer Sauza, who claims to have a lead on a cache of the near-mythical psychedelic drug known as Symphony 49. But no sooner has Ruiz returned from her sojourn at the Echo Hotel and taken her seat next to Smiley than *three* Palmer Sauzas show up in the space of a couple minutes. Three identical versions of the same guy, from three different parallel realities, each of whom has apparently spent his whole life under the impression that he's the only Palmer Sauza in the interdimensional smuggling business. Put too many people with Weird Luck together in one place, and this is exactly the kind of shit that happens.

Running into versions of oneself from other realities is an occupational hazard of interdimensional travel, especially for those with Weird Luck, and there's a type of person who can take that sort of thing in stride. Palmer Sauza, unfortunately, seems to be the opposite of that type, and an ugly vibe of There-Can-Be-Only-One quickly develops between the three of him. Smiley, who's so adept at taking weird events in stride that the Reality Patrol shrinks are starting to worry about him, steps in and tries to smooth things over by pretending to be a member of Flammarion's crew. Not a bad move in theory, but Smiley's announcement that he's Flammarion's authorized representative—an announcement delivered rather loudly, because that's what it takes to get the attention of these three Palmer Sauzas—is overheard by a group of bounty hunters who got wind of tonight's deal and came here to grab any member of Flammarion's crew they could get their hands on.

At this point, the mission goes sideways fast. As Weird Luck would have it, though, Ruiz and Smiley come out of the whole fiasco looking pretty good. They don't nab Flammarion, but it's clearly not their fault, and they do manage to make it back to Denebola Base with the sole surviving Palmer Sauza in custody. With the intel they get out of Sauza, the Reality Patrol is able to retrieve that cache of Symphony 49 before it falls into presumably less responsible hands—a success for which Ruiz and Smiley end up getting much of the credit. Between this fortuitous turn of events and the delicious memories of her time with Madeline, Ruiz is riding high for a good forty-eight hours or so before the inevitable complication arises.

•

The complication is Bianca. Bianca's been a fixture on Denebola Base since before Ruiz signed on with the Reality Patrol, and hasn't aged a day in all that time. Her job, which she performs with a level of skill that's become legendary, is to provide psychological counseling to agents suffering from post-traumatic stress and other psychological woes. Unofficially, her work also includes interrogation, and any other task to which the Reality Patrol decides her formidable telepathic talents might be suited; in fact, she's the one who got the location of all that Symphony 49 out of Palmer Sauza.

Rumors abound as to precisely what manner of entity Bianca might be, since she's clearly not human. Many an imaginative junior agent has pointed to her eternal youth and frost-white complexion as evidence she's a vampire, but Ruiz and Smiley know the truth is darker than that. They got the inside scoop years ago from their old superior Agent Jackson, who's the base's Chief of Security these days and has known Bianca longer than anyone. According to Jackson, Bianca's a lloigor, an ancient supernatural predator that feeds on the psychic emanations generated by human suffering. Captured by the Reality Patrol after some catastrophic mishap left her weakened and vulnerable, she was eventually deemed by the higher-ups to be "rehabilitated," whatever *that's* supposed to mean, and was subsequently assigned her current duties at her own request.

When Smiley first learned this, he was so intrigued that he approached Bianca and struck up a conversation, and over time the two of them have formed what he insists is a genuine friendship. But Smiley's never been a paragon of sound judgment, and Ruiz, who has grave doubts as to whether terms like "rehabilitated" and "friendship" can legitimately be applied to such a creature, has always preferred to give Bianca a wide berth.

Anyway, a couple days after the Cordova Spaceport mission and the recovery of the Symphony 49, Ruiz is in the Blackstar Lounge, the best nightspot on Denebola Base, listening to Smiley regale a few of their fellow agents with the Tale of the Three Palmer Sauzas. It's quite the epic, the way he tells it, full of sound and fury and dramatic reversals of fortune. When it comes to storytelling, Smiley treats actual events as mere launching points. It's becoming clear that they'll need more drinks; they've finished the first round and he hasn't even got to the part where the first Sauza shows up. Ruiz scans the room for a waiter, and that's when she spots Bianca.

Denebola Base is situated at a nexus in deep space where multiple realities meet, and one wall of the Blackstar is a massive window looking out on an ever-shifting vista of overlapping starscapes. Bianca's at her usual table, right at the foot of that transparent wall. Glass of wine at her elbow, back turned to the rest of the room, motionless as she takes in the view. Ruiz sees Bianca sitting there and all at once it hits her that there's no way to keep her tryst with Madeline a secret from a telepath of that caliber. If the stories she's heard from Jackson and Smiley are to be believed, Bianca's able to listen in on the thoughts of everyone around her at once, pretty much all the time.

Fuck. Madeline may be nothing more sinister than a fun-loving book thief, but her association with the Order of Eight Directions still makes her a terrorist in the eyes of the Reality Patrol. If Ruiz's superiors find out she's been having kinky funtime with a wanted interdimensional terrorist, and that she seems to have developed some inconveniently serious feelings for said terrorist, they'll see her as irredeemably compromised and she can kiss her career goodbye.

No, not just her career. Her whole fucking *life*. They'll throw her in an interrogation cell and squeeze every drop of information out of her, every intimate detail, then ship her off to die in a labor camp while they go after Madeline. And of course, to make sure Ruiz can't keep a single secret, they'll set Bianca loose on her—Bianca, who'll delight in every second of Ruiz's despair and humiliation and ruin, cause she's a fucking lloigor and other people's suffering is her favorite meal. Which gives Bianca every reason to turn Ruiz in.

Fuck fuck fuck fuck *fuck*. She's got to get out of here. Bianca could be reading her mind *right fucking now*...

And at the exact instant Ruiz realizes it might already be too late, Bianca turns and looks directly at her, meets her gaze with dark inhuman eyes, and smiles.

•

Ruiz finds herself roaming the halls of Denebola Base, aimless and frantic, moving fast because if she slows down she'll completely lose her shit. She barely remembers stumbling out of the Blackstar. How long before they arrest her? Has Bianca reported her yet, or is that *puta malvada* taking her time? She needs to calm the fuck down and *think*.

She's got to get to the Echo Hotel. Even the Reality Patrol can't follow her there, if the hotel doesn't want them to. What was it Madeline said about intentional straying? *Find someplace strange, someplace a bit on the labyrinthine side, and let yourself wander.* Denebola Base is labyrinthine as it gets, but Ruiz was paying attention during Orientation, way back when she was a cadet, and knows there are ontological stabilizers built into the base's core that prevent anyone from straying into or out of this reality. Only way off Denebola Base is via an authorized interdimensional portal, calibrated by technicians from the Reality Patrol's Portal Technologies Division. Which means her only shot at reaching the sanctuary of the hotel is to hop an elevator to one of the base's portal bays, activate one of the portals that's already been set up for someone else's departure, and hope that when she jumps through that portal it turns out to lead somewhere weird and labyrinthine enough that she can stray from there to the hotel before the Reality Patrol catches up with her.

Security on those portal bays is tight, though. No way to pull this off without a diversion. And for that, she's going to need Smiley. Until tonight she's never had to ask herself whether any of the fellow agents she's come to count as friends would put loyalty to their friendship above loyalty to the Reality Patrol. Thinking about it now, she realizes Smiley's the only one. No one who knows him would describe Smiley as trustworthy, not in any conventional sense of the word, but somehow she knows she can trust him with *this*.

Back to the Blackstar, then. Denebola Security can track the location of anyone on the base, so there's no point staying out of sight. If she hasn't made it out of this universe by the time the arrest order goes out, she's equally fucked whether she's hiding in a crawlspace or strolling around in plain view.

Smiley's right where she left him, along with the other agents they were hanging with. And way over at the far end of the room, Bianca's still there, too, alone at her little table, dwarfed by that enormous window. She's reading a book now, and Ruiz feels a quick flutter of hope. If Bianca hasn't gone scurrying off to rat her out yet, and if Ruiz can get Smiley out of the Blackstar before Bianca notices she's back and goes snooping in her mind again, maybe it's still not too late for this escape plan to work.

Smiley spots her approaching and raises his half-full glass in greeting. "Ah, Ruiz! *There* you are. All well, I trust?"

"Sorry to pull you away," Ruiz says, "but something's come up." Use a line like that on a Reality Patrol base and no one asks questions; everyone assumes it's official business. Fifteen minutes later, Ruiz and Smiley are ensconced in a corner booth in one of the noisier dining establishments in the base's rest-and-recreation sector. The house specialties here are noodles, tea, and an incessant techno-pop soundtrack. The music's why they picked this place—a shield against prying ears as Ruiz leans forward across the table and spills the story of her Echo Hotel adventure, leaving out the naughty kinky bits but tearfully owning up to the fact that she's pretty damn sure she's in love.

Smiley's a champ about the whole thing. When the tears start, he surprises her by reaching out and taking hold of her hand. He listens in sympathetic silence till she gets into the part about how she needs to find a way off the base before Bianca turns her in.

"If I may venture an observation," he says, "to resign yourself to life as a fugitive at this point seems premature. It is by no means certain that Bianca has made up her mind to expose you. Perhaps, were you to take the matter up with her directly, the need for such drastic action might be averted by mutual agreement."

"You think I can fix this shit by, what, just walking up and *talking it out* with her? No way, man. You're out of your everfucking skull."

"Why not? Hundreds of our esteemed colleagues have spoken with her over the years, in her professional capacity, and by all accounts they've benefited from the experience."

"Yeah, but *she* benefits, too, cause she feeds on their pain while she's helping them! And when she rats me out, the bitch gets to feed on *my* pain!"

"Bianca has assured me in the past that her duties provide abundant opportunity to satisfy her appetites. She's hardly starving. Consider the possibility that exposing your indiscretion in order to feed on you is an indulgence she might be willing to forego, in service to other priorities."

Ruiz opens her mouth to argue further, but just then their noodles arrive. By the time the waiter has set the steaming bowls on the table and gone out of earshot again, Ruiz has had an insight: "Dammit, you're not just talking out your ass like usual. You *know* something, don't you? About Bianca's 'priorities'?"

"Naturally. After all, the good counselor and I have been friends for quite some time."

"Just so we're clear... you do understand she's an evil supernatural entity whose nature is to prey on humans?"

"People can change, old friend. You and I certainly have."

"Yeah, but is a thing like Bianca even a person?"

"Surely it behooves us to be broad-minded when it comes to the matter of personhood, given that a few minutes ago you told me you had a conversation with an extradimensional hotel. Please, I implore you, go speak with Bianca. She's likely still in the Blackstar; she's been known to read there for hours at a stretch."

"But..."

"No further buts, my dear Ruiz. Go! Seek her out and settle this at once, so that your mind may be at ease! For my part, it shall be my honor, as your loyal friend, to remain fearlessly at this table and ensure that none of these noodles go to waste."

•

So it's back yet again to the Blackstar, where sure enough Bianca is still engrossed in her book. Bianca's table, like the other tables positioned near the transparent wall, has instead of chairs a comfortably-cushioned semicircular bench, a seating arrangement which ensures that anyone dining this close to the famous view will be able to appreciate it without having to constantly turn their head. Bianca's seated dead center on the bench. Ruiz slides in on her right, aiming to get close enough for a quiet conversation, but Bianca picks this precise instant to lift her head, in a way that strikes Ruiz as distinctly reptilian, and stare straight into Ruiz's eyes again. Some primal mammalian instinct kicks in, a chorus of distant evolutionary ancestors suddenly in Ruiz's head shouting *Keep your distance, foolish descendant, that thing is not one of us*, and for half a second she's paralyzed. Then she rallies, overrides millions of years of evolutionary wisdom, and forces herself to sit, though it's too late to keep the moment from being awkward.

Fuck, say her primate ancestors.

"I'm sorry," Bianca says. Her voice is low and throaty. "I didn't mean to alarm you. Not just now, and not earlier this evening." Up close, that ghost-white face, with its bluish lips and black alien eyes, is disconcertingly pretty. She closes the book she was reading and puts it down on the table. Ruiz steals a glance at the title, but it's in Japanese. Her gaze shifts to Bianca's left hand, which is missing its pinky and ring fingers. The fingers, according to the story Ruiz heard from Agent Jackson, were cut off during Bianca's extended torture by Reality Patrol interrogators, in the months following her capture. Probably best not to stare.

Bianca sighs. "In the accident that led to my capture, I lost the ability to control people's minds. I still *read* minds as well as ever, but I can't make them do what I want. It used to be so easy. If I wanted someone to feel a particular way, I'd just reach into their mind with my own and make the change. Now I have to do it the way humans do, nothing but words and gestures and facial expressions. So clumsy, so much room for misinterpretation. No wonder most of you are so miserable."

She sounds genuinely sad. Ruiz didn't know what to expect from this conversation, but she sure as hell didn't expect *this*. After a few seconds, in which Ruiz fails to come up with anything to say, Bianca gives another sigh and continues. "When I smiled at you earlier, I meant it to be reassuring. A way of saying that your secrets are safe with me. But of course, it had the opposite effect. I really am sorry for that. I suppose I should've called out to you. Telepathically, I mean. I can still *speak* inside people's minds, that's different from *controlling* a mind. But the state you were in, I was afraid hearing my voice in your head without warning would panic you even further."

"You're saying... you're *not* going to turn me in?"

"I'm not going to turn you in. And to answer the next question you were preparing to ask, I'm not going to blackmail you, either. There's no catch here."

Ruiz lets out a long ragged breath and for a short time she's so overcome with relief that she just sits there staring out the big window, side by side with Bianca, feeling the anxiety drain out of her. But then, of course, the curiosity kicks in. "I... Hey, I appreciate that. Seriously. I mean, I guess you *know* how much I appreciate it, cause you're reading my mind and shit, but... Look, I gotta ask, why *not* rat me out? Seems like you'd have plenty to gain from it. Smiley says you've got other priorities, and lucky for me I guess he was right, but what the hell *are* they?"

"We need friends, Margarita."

It's been a long time since anyone but a lover addressed Ruiz by her first name, and the unexpected intimacy throws her off balance almost as much as the cryptic brevity of Bianca's answer. What's she mean by *we*, here?

Once again, Bianca answers before Ruiz asks the question aloud. "Underneath their technological marvels and their grand rhetoric about protecting the multiverse, the Reality Patrol is a brutal authoritarian organization dedicated to forcing reality itself to conform to a set of arbitrary norms and limits. And *look* at us, Margarita. Look at you and me, and Smiley, and others like us. You play the role of the hard-boiled special agent so well, but behind the façade you've still got the heart of the strange sensitive little dreamer you were as a kid, even if it took falling in love with Madeline to remind you. Smiley is a quixotic mountebank who remains alive only by virtue of Weird Luck, and because friends like you and I keep quiet about it each time he hoodwinks his superiors. And according to my personnel file, I'm not even technically a *person*. We manage to survive, against all odds, within an organization that has as its ultimate goal a multiverse in which weird anomalies like ourselves no longer exist. It's a precarious situation, as you realized just this evening, and in the long run the only way we stand a chance is if we learn to recognize each other, and help each other as best we can."

"Whoa," Ruiz says. "And here I thought you were some sorta embodiment of pure evil."

"Perhaps I am, by human standards. I relish the pain of others, and I suppose I always will. Not because I bear anyone any malice, mind you. It's just my nature. But I've been a captive here on Denebola Base thirty years, and spent more than twenty of those years helping your fellow agents heal from psychological trauma even as I struggle to heal from my own, and it's changing me."

"Hunh. Changing you into what?"

"I wish I knew."

"Yeah, well, I admit I'm biased here, but I'd say this whole not-ratting-me-out thing makes you a better person than, like, ninety percent of humans."

"Thank you."

"Heh. *What* did you call me before? A 'strange sensitive little dreamer?'"

"You can't hide the truth from a lloigor."

"Guess not."

They sit for a while and watch the stars.

•

Four days later Ruiz is back in the field, partnered not with Smiley but with another old comrade-in-arms, Agent Kwon. The mission this time takes them to New York City, on some version of 21st-century Earth where the timeline has veered off in a radically different direction from the one in which Ruiz was born. She's seen a lot of Earths over the past couple decades; hasn't kept count but it's gotta be at least fifty or sixty by now. Maybe a dozen New York Cities, no two of them alike. This is one of the ugly ones. Teeming slums extend underground into networks of decommissioned subway tracks, immense black skyscrapers loom against a perpetually smoke-clouded sky. Major cyberpunk dystopia vibes, bleak as all fuck. But if the key to finding her way back to Madeline is to get herself lost somewhere strange and labyrinthine, well, here's her chance. Soon as she and Kwon are checked into their adjoining rooms, in a towering hotel that's respectable by local standards but of course can't hold a candle to the good old Echo, Ruiz announces she's going out for a while to get to know the city.

The selection of gadgetry she's equipped with, for this particular mission, includes a personal cloaking field that renders the user invisible to the human eye, and a cybernetic phone implant with some high-end GPS technology that would be mighty useful if she *didn't* want to get lost. First thing she does when she hits the street is duck into a shadowed doorway for a moment to switch the cloaking field on and the GPS off. Then she's away into the night, choosing, at each opportunity, whichever direction seems like it will lead deeper into obscurity and further from anyplace reputable enough to be marked on a map.

Takes her less than forty-five minutes to end up in a maze of subterranean tunnels with no clue how to get back to the surface. People live down here, whole neighborhoods built up over generations from salvaged materials, lit with power siphoned from the grid of the city above. Ruiz keeps to the outskirts, steering clear of the lighted areas; the vision-enhancing tech embedded in her Reality-Patrol-issue sunglasses lets her see perfectly well in the dark, albeit only in shades of gray.

Now that she's good and lost, she lets her mind drift to thoughts of Madeline and the Echo Hotel, and her feet wander wherever they will. She weaves her way aimlessly, humming to herself, pretending she's drunk. Presently she notices that the walls around her are smoother and cleaner, the ground beneath her boots more even. Next corner she turns, she's looking at a slightly wider passage, and a dozen yards down it on her left there's a single dim light set in an antique-looking metal wall fixture. Up ahead the path intersects another and continues onward into darkness, but before she reaches the intersection her attention's caught by an innocuous little door set in a shallow recess in the wall to her right, directly opposite the light fixture. She tries the knob and the door opens easily, revealing a long straight hallway, perfectly clean, lit by softly-glowing orbs suspended from the ceiling. She takes off the dark-vision sunglasses and sees that the walls of the hallway are painted robin's-egg blue. At the far end is another door, polished wood with brass fittings. A subtle shift her visual field as she steps into the hallway lets her know that her personal cloaking field is no longer active, and she remembers that Reality Patrol tech doesn't work in the Echo Hotel. She grins and breaks into a run.

The door this time leads directly into the Echo Hotel's majestic lobby. Behind the front desk, the same cheerful red-uniformed echo who delivers the room service carts materializes out of thin air. "Welcome back, Agent Ruiz."

"Hey, Hotel. Lookin good. Madeline around?"

"Thank you, ma'am. Miss de Verninac is in the library. Shall I inform her of your arrival?"

"Nah, I'll surprise her."

•

In the library, Ruiz finds Madeline cross-legged on a chair at a table piled with books, wearing one of those cozy hotel bathrobes, hair fallen forward to hide her face as she studies the volume open in front of her. So perfectly adorable, absorbed in her reading, that Ruiz would be content to just stand here watching her for hours. But Madeline senses her presence right away, glances up and lets out this long high-pitched squeal, *"Eeeeeeee!"* as she scampers right over the table, knocking books in all directions, and hurls herself into Ruiz's arms.

Vigorous kissing ensues, till Ruiz contrives to work the robe free of Madeline's shoulders and abruptly pull it downward. Madeline, who's wearing nothing underneath, squeals again. Ruiz grabs handfuls of robe, thwarting Madeline's efforts to disentangle her arms from the sleeves, and takes this opportunity to go to work with her mouth on Madeline's slender ticklish neck until Madeline manages to wriggle her way out of the robe entirely. This is the part where the troublesome little minx inevitably makes a break for it and needs to be chased down, but Ruiz is ready this time and tackles her before she can get started. More squealing, as Ruiz uses the bathrobe's belt to tie Madeline's elbows together behind her back. "Shhh," Ruiz says. "This is a library."

"This is hardly fair," Madeline pouts, once her arms are secured and Ruiz has helped her stand up again. "You didn't even give me a running start."

Ruiz pulls her close for a long kiss, then gives her a sharp smack on the butt. "Okay," she says. *"Now* you can run."

•

In bed one time, basking in that post-orgasm glow, Madeline with crossed wrists still tethered to the headboard and feet to the bedposts, Ruiz lounging beside her, Madeline makes with that mischievous smile and says, "You know, we could play like this forever, me the captive and you my captor, and I'd never get tired of it."

"Glad you feel that way, cause I'm planning on keeping you."

"Mmm. But listen, hon, I want you to know, my sense of fun's versatile as it is wicked. What really matters isn't the position I'm playing, just that it's *you* I'm playing with. So if you ever want to change things up and put yourself at *my* mercy, I promise you it would be every bit as enjoyable and satisfying for me as *this* is."

Now, here's a secret about Ruiz: all through the long rickety roller coaster ride of her pre-Madeline dating history, she's only ever been the top. In the rich and vivid world of her private fantasies, though, she's cast herself in a submissive role more often than not. Her bottomish proclivities have been confined to the realm of imagination partly because her hardass exterior keeps attracting partners who are looking to get topped, and partly because, let's be honest here, Ruiz has some major trust issues and the prospect of making herself so vulnerable scares the shit out of her. No surprise, then, that Madeline's offer triggers a hot flush of excitement Ruiz can't entirely hide.

Madeline's smile gets downright evil. "Yes," she says, "I think I'd enjoy myself quite a bit."

Luckily, despite all this big talk of turning the tables, the impertinent brat is still bound splayed out on the bed, which puts Ruiz at somewhat of an advantage when it comes to shutting down this unnerving line of speculation. A quick swing of her leg and she's sitting astride Madeline's slender torso. "I bet you would," she says. "But it's not gonna happen." With the thumb and forefinger of each hand, she takes hold of Madeline's nipples and gives a good hard pinch. Madeline squeaks. Ruiz grins down at her and pinches a little harder. "Let's make sure you don't forget your place again. Do you promise to be a good girl from now on?"

"Never!"

"I was hoping you'd say that..."

Later, with a properly chastened Madeline sleeping contentedly beside her, Ruiz lays on her back, crosses her wrists up near the top of her head, pretends they're tied like that. Imagines Madeline astride her, looking down at her with that diabolical smile. Could she dare let Madeline take charge?

If only. But that whole fear of vulnerability thing isn't the only complicating factor. Ruiz has lived too long in the world of interdimensional espionage to dismiss the possibility she's being played, the chance this is all some monstrously cruel Order of Eight Directions scheme to compromise and blackmail a Reality Patrol agent. It's a slim chance, for sure. Not the Order's style, not consistent with the data on Madeline. Plus, all her life Ruiz has had this uncanny instinct, give her a little time with someone and she can always tell what sort of shit they can or can't be trusted with. Never steered her wrong yet, and this instinct tells her Madeline would never hurt her, at least not on purpose. But even if the chance of betrayal's only one in a million, she can't pretend it's zero.

And if this *is* all a trick, if somehow the hotel's rigged up with hidden cameras and microphones or something, Ruiz knows that footage of her all bound and submissive would humiliate her infinitely more than footage in which she's the top. This whole thing with Madeline is a calculated risk, and the bottom line, so to speak, is that switching roles even briefly would push the level of risk into the unacceptable. So, yeah, not gonna happen.

•

Her concerns with risk management don't change the fact Ruiz is head over heels in love, a love which far as she can tell is enthusiastically reciprocated. It's more than just their kinks that are compatible. In between erotic escapades, during meals and hot tub soaks and time spent laying around in each other's arms, they find themselves immersed in conversation, enchanted with one another in every way. Ruiz tells Madeline about growing up in one of those dismal versions of late 20th century America where some seriously bad shit could happen if people found out you were queer. About her parents finding out and ejecting her from their house on a freezing winter night when she was fifteen, last time she ever saw them and also the same night she first experienced interdimensional travel.

"Where I come from," Ruiz says, "the scumbags who made everything suck for the rest of us were mostly racist homophobes. And the Reality Patrol, funny thing is, they *aren't* racist homophobes, so I figured they must be the good guys. They gave me a life where I got to do the cool sci-fi spy movie shit I daydreamed about as a kid, *and* be out of the closet without fear. Made it way too easy to overlook the part where they're basically a bunch of authoritarian uber-cops. Kinda hard to ignore that shit *now*, though, cause I can't stop thinking about what they'd do to *you* if they got the chance."

Madeline, for her part, will speak freely and at length about any topic *except* her own past. Funny thing to be reticent about, given that she seems to have no other boundaries or filters whatsoever. Ruiz doesn't push, though. Truth is, she's had a peek at Madeline's Reality Patrol file, so she already knows more about her quirky lover's history than she lets on. She knows, for instance, that Madeline, who like so many interdimensional travelers has skipped around in time as well as between realities, was born into a family of minor European aristocrats on some relatively unremarkable version of Earth in the year 1754. She also knows that Madeline was only nine years old when she vanished from her native timeline, perhaps as a result of inadvertently straying into the Archive.

Has she been a member of the Order of Eight Directions since the age of nine? That would explain a lot, including maybe this whole unwillingness to discuss her past. If her life's been that entwined with the Archive and the lives of other members of the Order, could be there's no way for her to talk about it without giving away information the Order wouldn't want any Reality Patrol agent to have. Then again, not talking about the past could be just another of

Madeline's myriad eccentricities. Madeline's own explanation is just the sort of thing Ruiz has come to expect from
her. "Why dwell on who I *used* to be? Who I am *now*, with
you, is my favorite me, and the past is my least favorite
thing to be tied to. Besides, if you want to know the heart of
a scholar, don't ask where they came from, ask what they're
interested in."

"Okay, you adorable little nerd, what are you interested
in?" A question which could lead to some troubling places,
since one reason the Reality Patrol is after Madeline's ass
is her reputed penchant for the sort of arcane knowledge
that in the wrong hands leads to titanic and amorphous
god-things from outside ordinary spacetime materializing
in the middle of cities. Turns out, though, that what Madeline's studying these days, and will eagerly enthuse about
for hours, is butterflies. She's hatching a plan to create a
butterfly sanctuary here in the hotel, but wants to learn
everything possible on the topic first. "Think about it," she
says. "It can be a perfectly controlled environment here,
safe from the vicissitudes of planetary weather or human
technology."

"And how's the hotel feel about you filling her with butterflies she's gotta help take care of?"

"Hey, it's a form of hospitality."

•

It's less heartwrenching, this time, to take her leave and
get back to the rest of her life, because now Ruiz knows she
really can find her way back to Madeline on her own. She

steps through a doorway in the Echo Hotel's lobby and appears in her room in that vastly inferior hotel in dystopian cyberpunk New York. Rest of the week, as she and Kwon carry out their mission—a bit of routine espionage and sabotage, making sure a certain corporation fails to develop an artificial intelligence capable of merging with other versions of itself in parallel realities—Ruiz is in the best of spirits. "How are you in such a good mood?" Kwon wants to know. "You hate realities like this even more than you hate every other sort of reality we get sent to."

"Oh, yeah, this place sucks. Guess I've just got a song in my heart."

"Well, that explains the incessant cheerful humming. It's like being on a mission with Smiley."

The mission's a success, everything seamless, and before they head back to Denebola Base she wanders off into the city one more time to find the Echo Hotel again. This time it's noticeably easier, no more than twenty minutes before she's back in Madeline's arms. They hang out and play for what feels like another three or four days before Ruiz says *hasta luego mi amor* and rejoins Kwon for the return trip to Denebola Base. Kwon's none the wiser; from his perspective, she's been gone less than half an hour.

•

Life keeps getting better. At some point or another in almost every mission, and each time she's away from Denebola Base on leave, Ruiz finds opportunities to slip off to the Echo Hotel for what seems like only minutes or seconds to everyone else, but for her and Madeline is long glorious stretches of luxuriating in one another's company. She introduces Madeline to the music that got her through her teen years and continues to feel like the soundtrack of her soul; Madeline's delighted by all of it and treats Ruiz to an extensive tour of her own eclectic musical interests, which range from elaborate orchestral and choral compositions, to ballads and showtunes from dozens of wildly disparate universes, to joyous *a cappella* pieces involving what sounds like hundreds of voices. The butterfly sanctuary project continues to move along. Ruiz embarks on a project of her own, teaching herself the fine art of rope bondage, learning to immobilize Madeline with ever-more-intricate webs of creative knotwork, in a variety of positions selected for their aesthetic appeal and amusing indignity.

Meanwhile, she's enjoying her off-duty hours on Denebola Base in a way she never has before. Those excursions to the Echo Hotel not only keep her in a constant good mood but also imbue her with an air of easy warmth that makes people seek out her company. So, yeah, life's pretty damn sweet, till one night she's shooting pool with Kwon and some other off-duty agents when Smiley walks in. He heads straight for her, face carefully neutral, ominous behavior in a guy who's normally incapable of crossing a room without greeting everyone he passes. "Sorry to pull you away," he says, "but something's come up."

She follows him out of the pool hall, around a couple of bends that lead them away from the main concourse of this area of the base, and finally into a vacant out-of-the way restroom. "I'll come right to the point," he says, soon as the door closes behind them. "Madeline de Verninac's been arrested by the Reality Patrol."

Ruiz's face and hands have gone suddenly numb, and some small part of her that feels very far away thinks about the expression *the color drained from her face* and wonders if this is what it feels like when that happens. Like all the blood in her body has recoiled from the world and become a hard clot in the middle of her stomach. Smiley's got one hand on her shoulder, but she can't feel it. He's still talking. "She's here on the base, in isolation. Ran afoul of one of Agent Xax's operations. She wasn't the target, but Xax's team saw an opportunity to grab her and they took it. Xax was itching to question her himself, but I got wind of the situation and intervened. I pointed out to our superiors that a member of the Order of Eight Directions merits interrogation by the most powerful telepath we have on hand, meaning Bianca of course, and that Xax's methods were likely to traumatize the prisoner in ways which could make Bianca's job harder. My argument won the day. Xax is livid, but Madeline's safe from him for the moment."

"I need to see her." The words sound small and distant, like they're not hers, like they're coming from somewhere outside her.

"They're not letting anyone see her till Bianca's had time with her."

"I need to talk to Bianca."

"Quite so. Bianca will no doubt be in her office. She'll have only just got word of this matter herself; she'll need time to review Madeline's files."

•

Bianca opens the door to her office a few seconds before Ruiz reaches it. "Margarita," she says. "Come in." No surprise Bianca sensed her approaching; to a being who feeds on distress, right now Ruiz probably smells the way a raw steak smells to a panther. Bianca guides her to the couch and sits down with her. On the coffee table is a stack of file folders, Madeline's name clearly visible on the one at the top. Ruiz's anguish must be a feast for Bianca, maybe it's even getting her high, but you wouldn't know it from the gentle concern on Bianca's face. Ruiz struggles for words, then looks into those strange dark eyes and realizes she doesn't need words at all; Bianca sees into her soul, picks up on every thought, knows exactly how helpless and terrified and lost she feels.

Next thing Ruiz knows, Bianca's holding her and she's bawling, crying full blast like she hasn't since she was a little kid, tears drenching Bianca's shoulder. Bianca just stays with her, silent and infinitely patient, as the bawling gives way to deep shuddering sobs that go on and on and on. When the sobbing has finally passed, at least for now, Bianca says, "Margarita, I'll have to go, soon, to see Madeline. I want you to know, first of all, that I'll be as gentle with her as the situation allows. While I play the sinister interrogator for the benefit of the recording devices in the interrogation room, secretly I'll be speaking to her in her head, comforting her as best I can."

This brings on another wave of sobbing. "Thank you," Ruiz manages to say.

"Of course. I told you I was going to be your friend, and I meant it. Which brings us to the second thing I need you to know: when I make my report about what I find in Madeline's mind, there'll be no mention of you or her relationship with you."

"Thank you, Bianca. For all of this."

"Third, I see in your mind that you're already thinking you might be able to save her somehow, to get her off the base and make a run for the Echo Hotel. Maybe you can. Maybe her Weird Luck combined with yours will allow you to beat the odds. I hope so. But this brings me to the final thing I feel I should tell you, which I'm afraid may not be so comforting. Madeline's in deep trouble, and not just because she's a member of the Order of Eight Directions. She was captured in the act of stealing classified information on the Corvus Drive."

Ruiz pulls away from Bianca and stares at her. Every agent's heard of the Corvus Drive, the ancient technomagical artifact which holds unparalleled power to alter the fabric of reality and the boundaries between universes, but which is so unstable that every attempt to use it has resulted in large-scale catastrophe. The Reality Patrol's been trying for generations to get hold of it and lock it up somewhere so it can't damage the multiverse any further, but the damned thing generates a field of Weird Luck that thwarts all attempts at containment. "No way," Ruiz says. "The fuck she was. The fucking *Corvus Drive?* That's supervillain shit. Necromancer shit, power-mad corporate CEO shit. That's not Madeline."

Bianca gestures toward the file folders stacked on the coffee table. "It's not Madeline as *you* know her. But it's entirely consistent with the profile of her in our files. Fascinated by occult secrets and dark mystical powers. Prone to obsession. Insufficient regard for the consequences of her actions."

"Fuck the files! They've got it wrong! Just more paranoid Reality Patrol bullshit, like how everyone who stands up to them gets labeled a fucking terrorist!"

"We'll know the truth once I've looked into Madeline's mind. But take it from someone who's spent centuries upon centuries seeing into the psyches of those around me: each person is more complex and multifaceted than even their most intimate companions usually know."

"No. Madeline, she's not... She... she likes butterflies..."

Bianca gives Ruiz's shoulder a gentle squeeze, then gets up and walks across the room to a desk in the corner. Opens a drawer, pulls out a small plastic container, fishes around in it, comes back over to Ruiz and hands her a little yellow pill. "Sedative. Take it. It will help you get through the next few hours. Go back to your quarters and get some rest. I need to go see Madeline now, and after that I'll have to make my report to our superiors immediately. But as soon as I can get back to this office again, I promise I'll send for you right away and tell you what I've learned, and we can talk about what to do next."

•

The sedative really does help. Once it kicks in, all the fear and worry about what's going to happen to Madeline seem like they've been taken out of Ruiz's head and placed in some adjacent space she can look at but not touch. Like her feelings are fish in an aquarium. She lays down in her bunk, falls asleep, and dreams about schools of fish that are also butterflies, until she's awakened by the message alert telling her Bianca's ready to see her. She's slept about six hours. Sedative hasn't fully worn off yet, but the anxiety's starting to creep back in. She gets herself to Bianca's office fast as she can, doesn't even bother trying to make herself presentable.

Bianca once again opens the door a moment before Ruiz gets there. Guides her to the couch but this time, instead of joining her there, curls up in an armchair across from her. There's something about Bianca that's changed, some new vitality, something feline and sensual about the way she's moving.

"Yes," Bianca says, doing that thing where she replies to an unspoken thought. "I've eaten well."

Takes a second for the implications to sink in, then it's only the last lingering effects of the sedative that keep Ruiz from leaping to her feet. "You said you'd be *gentle*! You said you'd fucking *comfort* her!"

Bianca raises a hand. "Wait. Listen. I *did* try to comfort her. I *did* keep it gentle, at first. But then I discovered something I hadn't anticipated: Madeline de Verninac has never heard of you, much less met you or been your lover."

Ruiz stares at her, uncomprehending.

"And yes," Bianca says, "I'm certain. And no, there's no magic or psychic power that could enable her to hide her memories from me. My skills are more than a match for such trickery."

"No. Fuck this shit. This can't..."

"Margarita. Listen. This is *good* news. The unfortunate woman we have in custody is not your Madeline."

Not her Madeline. Ruiz exhales loudly, shoulders slumping, tension draining from her body. "Not Madeline? But *how?* What the fuck is happening?"

"I'll tell you what I learned from her mind. The woman I just questioned is exactly the Madeline de Verninac who's described the Reality Patrol's files: a child of aristocrats who found her way into the Archive at the age of nine and grew into an accomplished occult scholar prone to unhealthy fixations, with tendencies far darker than the Madeline you know. A few years ago, while attempting to locate the Corvus Drive, she encountered the interdimensional pirate Rissa Flammarion, and the two of them became lovers."

"Wait, *what?*"

"Many of their passionate trysts took place in the Echo Hotel. In addition to their sexual chemistry and highly compatible kinks, de Verninac and Flammarion shared an ambition to possess the Corvus Drive, and were working together to locate it. But they were both volatile personalities, and the relationship ended badly. De Verninac did not deal well with the heartbreak. She never returned to the Echo Hotel. Her obsession with the Corvus Drive became all-consuming. In her determination to find it before Flammarion, she grew increasingly reckless, which in time led to her arrest and her present captivity."

"So you're saying we're dealing with two different versions of Madeline? Like, from two parallel realities? Two

Madelines who both had enough Weird Luck to find the Echo Hotel? I mean, that shit *happens*, right? Like when me and Smiley met those three versions of that smuggler guy who hadn't known about each other."

"Yes, such things *do* happen, especially when Weird Luck is involved. But in this case, there's another explanation which is far more in line with the facts as we know them."

"Okay, you lost me. What else could possibly explain this shit?"

Bianca smiles. It's probably meant to convey sympathy, but the effect is unsettling. "You already know. Some part of your mind has already figured out the truth, but other parts have been working hard to keep you from looking at it. Denial is such a fascinating phenomenon, don't you think? But now that I've brought it to your attention, I suspect you won't be able to keep the knowledge out of your awareness for even another minute."

"I have no idea what you're..."

And then it hits her.

"Oh," she says. "Oh, shit."

Bianca watches her, silent and still, like lizard or a cat.

"Fuck," Ruiz says. And then, a little while later, she says, "I need to deal with this *now*. Can't wait for my next mission. Need you to write me a note, in your capacity as a shrink. Recommend a couple days' emergency mental health leave, so I can go someplace where I can get to the hotel."

"Of course."

·

Another one of those little yellow pills gets her another six hours of sleep. By the time she's had breakfast and a shower, the request for emergency leave's been approved and there's a portal waiting to take her to a version of New York City far nicer than the last one she visited, on an Earth not too different from the one she grew up on. The main branch of the New York Public Library is a few stories taller in this reality than in most. Perfect place to get lost. Ten minutes wandering the stacks on the seventh floor and she's strayed out of New York and into the lobby of the Echo Hotel.

The perky young echo in the red uniform appears behind the front desk. "Agent Ruiz! Always a pleasure to have you here. Would you like me to ring Miss de Verninac?"

"Don't bother." She takes a quick look around and spots a place in one corner of the lobby where two big brown leather armchairs are facing each other, just a few feet apart. She sits down in one of them and gestures at the other one. "Come here," she says. "Sit."

The echo comes dancing across the marble floor and sits facing Ruiz, spine straight, wearing her habitual cheery smile. "Hello! What can I do for you, ma'am?"

"You can drop the act. I figured it out. Madeline's an echo. You're Madeline, Madeline's you, you're both just the Echo Hotel wearing different disguises."

For a second, the red-uniformed echo ripples like she's a reflection in a pool and something's disturbed the surface of the water. And then it's Madeline sitting there, dressed the exact same way she was when Ruiz first met her, hands clasped nervously in her lap, searching Ruiz's face with those beautiful emerald eyes. "I'm sorry," she says.

"Why'd you do it? Why'd you pretend to be the real Madeline?"

"At first? Because I was desperately horny. And then because I'd fallen in love with you, and I was afraid you'd leave me if you found out I wasn't human and that I hadn't been honest with you."

"I thought echoes had no minds of their own."

"They don't. I'm the hotel, just like you said. I'm so sorry. I never meant to hurt you."

"You're the hotel. And... you're in love with me?"

"Yes."

Ruiz stands up and steps over to the Madeline echo. Holds out her hand and the echo takes it, looking anxious and confused. Ruiz pulls the echo to her feet and kisses her, long and deep. After a while they get their tongues out of each others mouths long enough to catch their breath and look into each other's eyes. "You're not leaving me?" the echo says.

"Nah." More kissing ensues, and then they just stand there holding each other for a bit. "No one *ever* loved me," Ruiz says. "Not really, not the way I needed. Not the kinda love where people treat each other right. And now a whole fucking self-aware *universe* loves me? And wants to make me amazing food and have hot kinky sex with me? Why the hell would I ever walk away from *that?*"

"I was so scared of losing you. I was scared you wouldn't be able to love me if you knew I wasn't really a person."

"As a possibly insane but surprisingly smart friend of mine put it recently, it behooves us to be broad-minded when it comes to the matter of personhood."

"Ooh, I like that."

"Yeah, but... what do I even *call* you now? 'Madeline' doesn't seem right anymore, especially since it turns out the real Madeline de Verninac is kinda fucked up."

"Call me Echo."

After a little more kissing, they pull away just slightly and stand face-to-face, hands resting on one another's shoulders, and Ruiz says, "So, how'd a nice self-aware universe like you end up such a hot, horny, kinky little slut, anyway?"

Echo giggles. "A lot of people have sex in hotels. I get to watch all the sex that happens in my rooms, and over time I got *into* it. Looked so fun that I started using my echo bodies to fool around with some of the guests myself. Most guests don't know that the echoes are all just little old me; I let them go on thinking that each echo's a human member of the hotel staff. Sometimes if a guest seemed to be attracted to one of my echoes, I'd see what happened if that echo showed up at the door of their room without much clothing on."

"Holy porn movie plot, babe!"

"Hee! Aren't I just the naughtiest? Anyway, I'd been having that kind of sexy fun for a while when Madeline and Rissa came along. I'd seen guests get kinky before, but this was a whole new level. All BDSM, all the time. It was an awakening for me. Hottest thing I'd ever seen. I was so sad when they broke up. And I knew I had to find a playmate who'd be up for that kind of fun with *me*. But even when a guest was up for trying something kinky with one of my echo-forms, it wasn't the same. The chemistry between the partners has to be right. So for a while, I wasn't just a kinky horny hotel, I was a sexually frustrated hotel."

"Poor thing!"

"Shh, I'm just getting to the good part! I figured out ages ago how to send my echo bodies into other universes. Using my echoes to visit human worlds and learn about human cultures is how I turned myself into the magnificent hotel you see around you. So when I heard the rumor that Rissa would be showing up at that bar in the Cordova Spaceport Complex, I had a really bad idea. I'd make an echo-form for myself that looked just like Madeline, and I'd go meet Rissa at the bar and see if I could get her to come back and play with me the way she'd played with the original Madeline."

"Wow. That *was* a really bad idea."

"I know, right? In my defense, I was desperately horny. Fortunately, soon as I arrived in the bar, I saw *you*, and I just had this feeling about you. I could tell the chemistry was there. And you know the rest."

They take a long look at each other, just soaking it all in, and then Ruiz says, "So what do we do *now?*"

"Well, it was *ever* so naughty of me to hide the truth from you for so long..." Echo's smile has gone all impish and flirty.

Ruiz sighs. "Listen, babe. I know this is the part where I should punish you for being such a naughty girl, but I'm not sure I can get into it. I'm sorry. I love you. I'm not leaving you. It's just... I feel like... Shit, I don't even know how to explain."

"I understand," Echo says. Her voice is calm, but she looks stricken, almost panicked. "I messed this up. I get it if this is too weird for you. You're human, you need a lover who's a real human..."

"No! It's not that at all." Ruiz turns away, takes a deep breath. "I don't need you to be human. Shit, every human I've been with has let me down or fucked me over. And hey, you're not the real de Verninac, you're not Order of Eight Directions, that's actually a big load off my mind. And I love you, I love playing with you. It's just..." She sighs again, looks up at the vaulted ceiling, searching for the words.

Behind her, Echo is silent. The entire hotel is silent, a whole universe holding its breath. Ruiz begins again, slow and careful, trying to make it make sense. "I love playing with you. And you know I'm as kinky as you are. Never had a vanilla bone in my body. And the way we play, I mean... It's all consensual, of course, but... for me, I guess, I've always needed to be able to pretend it's less consensual than it is? Like, while it's happening, I need to feel like the game is for real, like my lover's truly in my power. Suspension of disbelief. I don't know, maybe there's something wrong with me, that I like it to feel so real."

"There's nothing wrong with you, Margarita. Believe me, I understand the appeal of getting into a kinky game all the way, making the sexy drama of captor and captive as real as you can. Madeline and Rissa were like that, too, and that's what made their play so exciting to watch and made me want to try it myself. I *love* how into it you are."

"But that's the problem," Ruiz says. "I tie up a human, sure, we both know I'll untie her if she signals that she really needs to stop—but long as she's tied up, she really *is* helpless. But you, you're this whole reality. You're basically a goddess.

The goddess, within your own borders. Omnipresent and pretty close to omnipotent. Complete control over all matter, at the molecular level, because you *are* all the molecules in this universe. Physical helplessness isn't *possible* for you. And now that I know this, how the hell can we ever go back to pretending you're in my power, even for a moment?"

Echo comes up behind Ruiz and puts a gentle hand on her back. "Oh, honey. *That's* what's bothering you? Don't you worry. We can fix this."

"Believe me, babe, I want to. More than anything. But I don't see how."

"Well, now that you know I'm not really a member of the Order of Eight Directions, or any kind of potentially untrustworthy human at all, you can finally take me up on my offer to switch roles and top *you* for a change."

Ruiz whirls to face her. Echo is smiling. It's suddenly become far too warm in here. Ruiz tries to say something, but words elude her and she just ends up swallowing nervously.

"Think about it," Echo says. "It's the perfect solution. Like you said, within my own borders I'm pretty much an all-powerful goddess. Suspension of disbelief will be easy, because you really *are* entirely at my mercy. The only thing protecting you right now from becoming my helpless plaything is that you haven't yet consented."

Ruiz can feel herself blushing. Fuck. She knows her arousal must be obvious.

"I should warn you," Echo says, "that if you do consent to me topping you, I have no intention of playing by human rules. You'll be in the power of a very cruel goddess. But we both know you *are* going to consent, because deep down you're a horny little submissive slut. So let's hear you give that consent, shall we?"

Ruiz licks her lips, swallows hard, and manages to whisper, "I consent."

Echo leans in and gives her a gentle kiss on the cheek. "I love you so much," she says.

The air shimmers and five more Madeline-echoes appear, each of them completely identical to the first. "I'm feeling generous," one of them says, "so I'll give you a running start."

Nick Walker is co-creator of the psychedelic urban fantasy webcomic *Weird Luck* (a collaboration with Andrew M. Reichart and Mike Bennewitz), which is part of a broader Weird Luck saga that also includes all of her prose fiction and Andrew M. Reichart's prose fiction. Her previous stories, which feature some of the same characters as "Ruiz and the Echo Hotel," have appeared in volumes 2, 3, and 5 of the annual neuroqueer lit anthology *Spoon Knife*. She's a queer transgender psychology professor who's somehow picked up a reputation as a leading thinker on neurodiversity, and her essay collection *Neuroqueer Heresies* is much more widely read than her fiction. Find her on Twitter at @WalkerSensei.

9 781945 955327